SAFARI

by

WILFRID ROBERTSON

LIST OF ILLUSTRATIONS

CONTENTS

CHAPTER ONE

FRANK HENSON put down his half-empty cup of muddy coffee and glanced out of the window. Beyond the deep shadows cast by the iron-roofed veranda lay a broad street and its background of low white buildings reflecting the slanting rays of the African sun. It was a morning full of sparkling life, as mornings at the beginning of the Rhodesian dry season always are; but little of its brightness reflected itself on Frank's young face.

There are many good hotels in Salisbury, the capital of Rhodesia, but the one in whose dining-room Frank sat was not among them. But it was the best he dared afford, for until he found a job he had only a few pounds in his possession, and he did not know how long these must be made to last.

As he tackled the bacon and toast, both of them limp and soggy, that a slouching native waiter had placed before him on the spotted and fly-blown table-cloth, he felt grimly certain that the kitchen from which they had come was equally repellent. However, he was hungry, and there was nothing he could do about it. Having finished, he lighted a pipe, and exchanged the cabbage-and-cheese smell of past meals that lingered in the dining-room for the purer air of the veranda outside.

The bedrooms, also on the ground floor, lay round the corner, and presently Frank went to the one that had been given him, picked up his sun-helmet, and wandered off down the street. He moved idly towards the centre of the town, and in time found himself strolling along the busy pavements of Manica Road, the main thoroughfare of Salisbury.

As he was passing the plate-glass frontage of a large shop he felt a tap on the shoulder. "Surely you're Henson?" said a voice.

The speaker was a middle-aged man clad in a well-cut suit such as are worn by townsfolk—a sharp contrast to the khaki shirt and shorts of the bush that formed Frank's garb.

"Yes, my name's Henson, but—" Frank paused. He seemed vaguely to recognise the other, but could not place him.

"Thought so. You don't remember me? We met when you first came out to this country three years ago. At the railway station, to be precise, just after you'd arrived."

Frank's face lit up. "Why, of course!" he exclaimed. "You're Mr. Larkman. I didn't recognise you for the moment." He held out a hand in eager greeting.

Frank remembered their first meeting with gratitude. There had been some trouble over his baggage, and the other, an old resident in the town, had spotted that he was in difficulty. Mr. Larkman had not only come to his rescue, but had taken the young man under his wing, and had spared time from his busy practice as a solicitor to fix Frank up with quarters, show him something of the town, and assist him generally.

"How have you been getting on all this time?" Mr. Larkman continued. "Look here, we can't talk in the street; let's go in yonder." He nodded towards a restaurant into which people were already drifting for the inevitable morning coffee.

They found a table, and the coffee was brought—very

different from the stuff that Frank had swallowed at breakfast—and the solicitor repeated his question.

Frank gave a slight shrug. "I've had my ups and downs," he admitted. "You remember I was going out as assistant on a farm? That failed, but I managed to get a job in the same district, well out in the wilds. That was fine while it lasted, for I got in a good deal of exploring round about, and shooting too, but like all good things, it came to an end."

"And what are you doing now?"

"Nothing," Frank replied ruefully. At the moment I'm looking for a town job of some sort. I hate the idea of it, after being out in the bush, but I've got to earn a living somehow. If I'd the capital I'd start a farm or something of that sort, but I haven't, so that's that."

Mr. Larkman set down his cup and put his fingers together.

"You were up north, or rather north-west, in the Gondi District, weren't you?"

"Yes."

"Do you know it well?"

"Not all, of course," Frank replied. "It's a pretty huge area." He went on to explain the parts he knew best.

The solicitor nodded. "Then I believe I can put you in the way of something you'll like. I have a client at the moment, a Mr. Mansfield, just out from England. He's a fellow a year or two older than you, perhaps, and he wants someone with bush experience as guide, helper, and companion on an expedition into those parts and beyond. How does the idea strike you?"

Frank's face lighted up. "It sounds too good to be true! What's he after—big-game shooting?"

"No, but I won't go into details now," Mr. Larkman replied, rising. "I must get back to work. What you'd better do, Henson, is to come round to my office to-morrow morning, say at ten o'clock, and I'll tell Mansfield to come, and you can go into the thing together. That suit? Right, I'll see you then. Where are you staying, by the way?"

Frank told him. The solicitor opened his eyes.

"That place—good heavens! Well, you seem to like roughing it!"

"I don't mind roughing it in the bush, but I don't like pigging it in a town," Frank replied with a laugh. "Still, I shan't mind it for another night or two if there's a chance of this job you speak about. I'll be along at your office on the stroke of ten, and I'm ever so grateful to you."

"You haven't got it yet," Mr. Larkman replied with a smile, and moved off down the street.

Though Frank was elated at the prospect of the kind of job he wanted, his natural caution warned him against counting too much upon it. For one thing, it would probably last only a short time; for another, he might find his prospective employer quite impossible. They would have to undergo the acid test of being continually in each other's company. However, it was a matter that could only be decided after he had seen him.

Frank reached the lawyer's office punctually the following morning, and a few minutes later the third man arrived.

As Mr. Larkman introduced them Frank ran a critical eye over Mansfield. He saw a young man a few years older than himself, with a reddish face and carroty hair, and dressed in clothes that had obviously been cut by a good tailor. Frank put him down as one who had lived a fairly easy life. He looked a bit soft physically, but that was to be expected, and a few weeks in the bush would soon harden him up. On the whole his appearance was favourable, though Frank's summing up received a slight setback at the offhand way Mansfield nodded when the solicitor introduced them. However, it was early yet to form a definite opinion.

The three sat down, and after a few general remarks Mr. Larkman put his elbows on the desk before him and placed his finger-tips together. He glanced at Mansfield. "Now we'd better get down to business," he said. "Will you explain the situation, or shall I?"

"Oh, I will." Mansfield lighted a cigarette, and as an afterthought passed the case to Frank. "I'd better start at the beginning," he went on. "It's like this. About six months ago a rich uncle of mine died, and he left his money in equal shares to myself and a cousin of the name of Oglethorpe. As the estate's a matter of £40,000, there's a good bit of money involved, see?

"Well, now, that looks simple on the face of it, but it isn't. You see, the old buffer was one of those would-be clever chaps who make their own wills, and he mucked up the wording. I don't remember exactly how it was put, but in essence it read that in the case of either legatee dying before he did, the money was to go to some charity affair that had got on the soft side of him. Obviously what he meant was the half-share of the one who'd died; but he worded it so infernally badly that it reads as if the whole of it was to go to this charity—which in my opinion is nothing better than a shady concern." Mr. Larkman held up a deprecating hand. "That's slander," he put in. "It's lucky that what is said here isn't likely to go any farther."

"It's a bogus concern, as you probably know as well as I do," Mansfield protested.

"Er, well, let's call it a charity of—er—doubtful

probity," Mr. Larkman amended. "Anyway, it's off the main point at present, so continue."

"Why, yes, that's true." Mansfield turned again to Frank. "We must go back a couple of years and come to my cousin Oglethorpe. He was a passenger in a plane travelling from England to Johannesburg, down south. It crashed in the district Mr. Larkman tells me you know, somewhere south of the Zambezi, and a lonely area, I understand."

"I seem to remember the incident," Frank commented. "There were a number of survivors, I believe, who started off on foot for the nearest outpost of civilisation."

"That's right, and Oglethorpe was among them. But on the second day he was found to be missing from the party, and since then nothing has been heard of him. This—er—esteemed charity"—Mansfield glanced at Mr. Larkman and grinned—"is trying to get his death presumed and, by the wording of that will, scoop both his share and mine. Meanwhile I'm open to bet he's no more dead than I am."

Frank shook his head. "I don't see how you make that out. If alive, he'd have turned up long ago. He'd have met natives, who'd have given him food and guided him. No, stands to reason he got hopelessly lost in the bush, and the hyenas and vultures would have made short work of his remains."

"But there's more to it than you think. Though he's my cousin, he's a fellow I've no use for; in fact, to put it bluntly, he's a rotter. There are no two ways about that. Always getting mixed up in shady affairs, besides having the deuce of a violent temper when annoyed. He took that plane trip on business, he said, but making a getaway would be nearer the mark. You see, a shady pal of his was found dead with a broken skull on a London pavement at 1 a.m., and the police suspected that Oglethorpe had chucked him there by way of a fourth-floor window. Later they reckoned the fall was accidental, but Oglethorpe couldn't know that—he'd gone by then. My reading is that he left that party of survivors deliberately, meaning to vanish and throw off pursuit. As he was never formally charged, no repeal was published, so no doubt he still thinks he's wanted, and is lying low somewhere."

"I see. That does put things in a rather different light," Frank admitted.

"Exactly. So I want to find him—not for his sweet sake, the blighter, but for my own. And I reckon the trail starts at the point where he left that party. You know the country. I don't. Are you willing to join me and organise the expedition?" He went on to speak of terms.

The salary offered was more than Frank would have cared to ask, and, despite his doubts at first, he felt that he and Mansfield might be able to shake down together without undue friction. But before coming to any decision he uttered a word of warning.

"I fancy it's going to be a tougher job than you expect," he said. "I don't know whether you realise that you'll have to stand up to a good deal of rough living and hard tramping—a bit different from what you've been used to, I expect."

Considerable surprise appeared on Mansfield's face. "Why so?" he asked. "I shall hire a car for the job, and from what I've seen from the train coming up from the coast, the roads don't look too bad."

Frank laughed. "You mustn't judge by what you've seen when journeying through the civilised parts. It's true we can go by car to the edge of the settled areas, but beyond that it's a case of tramping on our flat feet, with native carriers to handle our kit."

"But in these days—it's not the dark ages! Surely one can go anywhere by car nowadays?"

"Far from it, even to-day," Frank replied. "Though on a map Africa looks like a network of roads and railways, civilisation has spread only in strips, leaving huge areas of wild country in between. For instance, if I remember right, that plane crashed near a stream called the Swanswa, which must be fifty miles beyond the most primitive earth road. Don't forget the long tramp those survivors had before they got in touch with anywhere."

Mansfield shrugged his shoulders. "Well, I guess I can stick it as well as another. I'm game to try." He rose and picked up his hat. "You'll want to think over my offer—come and see me this afternoon with your answer." He named the comfortable hotel where he was staying, and held out a hand to Frank in a manner far more cordial than his earlier greeting. "I hope you'll accept," he added, and left the office.

Mr. Larkman and Frank glanced at each other. "Well?" asked the former, "what do you think of it?"

"I think he's banking on a slim chance. That country towards the Zambezi isn't London, where a chap can vanish among millions. There are no settlers or farms, and even a passing white man is a rarity; I can't see how this man Oglethorpe could be there long without a report of his presence filtering down through passing natives. However, there's always the unexpected, especially in Africa."

"That's so," Mr. Larkman agreed. "Meanwhile, what are you doing about his offer?"

"Oh, I shall accept and do my best for him—anything is better than hanging about here and the prospect of a town job. It won't be easy, for he's as soft as butter, and I shall probably get a peck of grousing when he finds what he's up against. But I expect he'll shake down to it in time."

"Treat him gently at first," said the solicitor with a smile, "or he'll insist on returning, and you'll get the sack, young man! After all, he'll be your employer."

"Quite so, but one or the other's got to do the organising, and he knows nothing about the bush. Now about expenses and my screw—I suppose he's all right for that? I shall have to buy a certain amount of stores and so on."

"You need have no fear on that score. I fancy he's fairly well off, despite his keenness about this disputed legacy. As a matter of fact I've seen his London banker's reference to the local branch of the Standard Bank here. I don't suppose you're likely to run him into anything unreasonable in the way of expenses."

"I certainly shan't. Nothing more fatal than trying to lug along a lot of stuff. More loads mean more native carriers to be signed on, and the more men means the more loads of meal you have to take to feed them. A vicious spiral, in fact. We'll have to depend largely on the country and native produce from the villages we strike; he's not going to find that cousin of his in a week or two, and he needn't think it."

"You must arrange these things as you think best," Mr. Larkman answered. "All that's quite beyond my province. Now, if you've decided to accept, you'd better go and find Mansfield and tell him."

"Yes, I will." Frank rose to his feet and after once more thanking the older man for his kindness, he emerged into the street. He waited for a moment until a gap in the passing traffic gave him a chance to cross over. He made his way in the direction of the public park, for he remembered that Mansfield had said, "Come and see me this afternoon," and it was still not yet 11.30. In the quiet and shady walks of the park he would have time to plan out the immediate future, and have a clear-cut scheme in his mind before calling at the hotel.

CHAPTER TWO

A COLD SCENT

MANSFIELD was seated in the crowded lounge of the hotel, idly turning over some illustrated papers, and he glanced up with something like eagerness as Frank entered. "Well, what's the verdict?" he asked.

"I'll take it on," Frank replied.

"That's good. I'm glad. Let's find somewhere where we can talk. Come up to my room, where we'll be out of this crush."

Together they left the lounge and passed up the wide stairs.

Mansfield motioned Frank to take the easy-chair, and seated himself on the bed. "Now we can be free from interruption."

After a few minutes of general discussion Frank came down to details.

"Since I saw you at the office I've been thinking things out. I propose to ring up a man I know, Kent by name, who has a farm in that direction—one of the farthest out, in fact. There's telephone line of sorts as far as his place provided it's not broken by a falling tree or the collapse of a rotten pole. He'll get hold of my old boss-boy Taka, and tell him to collect a gang of carriers to meet us there. He'll probably be in touch with several I've had before, and it will save a good deal of time."

Mansfield nodded agreement.

"About getting ourselves to Kent's place, I know of a

Ford truck I can hire, and I can get the loan of a coloured driver to bring it back."

"I'd prefer to hire a decent car and do it comfortably," Mansfield put in.

"Maybe, but you forget the load we'll have aboard— essential stores we've got to buy before leaving here. Besides, a posh car would cost three times as much— you're here to find a legacy, not to spend one," Frank added with a grin.

"I have my own blankets and rifle," he went on, "but you'll need both, I expect. What's that? Not going shooting? Yes, I know, but rifles are necessary, all the same; they've got to supply us with fresh meat as well as give protection from wild animals."

Mansfield remarked here that he had brought a revolver out from England.

"Then you can chuck it away," Frank retorted. "It's only an extra weight to carry, and quite useless for practical things. If you want to blot out anything, man or animal, use a rifle and make a decent job of it."

Mansfield laughed. "It seems I've a lot to learn," he said, and the admission made Frank more hopeful of their being able to settle down together. "Well now, will you see to the stores, and meanwhile give me a list of the kind of kit I shall need? These things, I suppose, will hardly do in the wilds," Mansfield added, glancing down at his neatly creased trousers and polished shoes.

Frank nodded agreement and turned to go, leaving Mansfield running his fingers through his carroty hair as he studied the brief list that had been scribbled out for him.

Two mornings later, shortly after sunrise, a battered truck pulled up outside the hotel. In it, beneath a crumpled sailcloth, lay Frank's roll of blankets and the stores he had bought. Frank himself climbed down from his seat beside the coloured driver and entered the building.

He had warned Mansfield of the need for an early start, but quite expected to find his employer still in bed. To his surprise, however, Mansfield had made an effort and was actually up, and it was not long before they were able to pull out.

As the cooler hours of the morning gave place to mid-day heat, so the roads over which they travelled changed also. The broad macadam of the capital gave place to parallel concrete strips, easy enough to run on as long as no other vehicles were met, but bumpy when one had to pull aside to pass.

Midday found them well on their way. They halted for an hour for a roadside meal, and then pushed on, presently reaching a small township where they stopped to fill up with petrol. Towards the late afternoon even the concrete strips had been left behind, and they were traversing beaten earth roads, raising a wake of dry-season dust that settled like fine flour on the bordering trees and foliage. Bridges, too, had vanished, and each stream-bed encountered had to be crossed by a rocky drift that made the truck's ancient springs squeal in protest.

Just before sunset they came in sight of Kent's lonely dwelling, a thatched building of sun-dried bricks flanked by the huts of his native employees on the farm. The truck drew up, and with their faces and clothing covered with a thick layer of powdery dust, Frank and Mansfield climbed stiffly down.

"Hallo, here you are!" Frank's friend emerged from the gathering shadows beneath the thatched veranda, and welcomed the travellers. He took them in and, while his house-boy lighted a paraffin lamp and began to place knives and forks on the home-made table, they had a much-needed drink and a wash.

Their bodily wants being satisfied and pipes alight, Kent began to talk. He had not seen another white man for weeks, and was full of chat; but presently Frank managed to head him off and turn the conversation to his own affairs.

Kent, he discovered, had got the carriers Frank had phoned about, and they were waiting down at the native quarters, ready for him to interview them in the morning. Taka had collected a dozen—was that enough? Frank reckoned it was, and went on to speak of the reason for the expedition, hoping to learn something from his host. But Kent knew nothing of any stranger in the wilds beyond him, and, as he pointed out, the spot where the plane had crashed was fifty miles away, so he would not be likely to know. Meanwhile Mansfield sat silent and yawning, surveying his host's primitive abode with a disparaging eye, and wishing he had brought something to rub on the bruises left by the seat of the bumping lorry.

Frank turned out next morning before the sun had risen, and in the pearly dawn found a dozen natives, with Taka at their head, waiting for him. A broad grin split Taka's black face as he saluted, and Frank noticed with satisfaction that his recruits looked a useful lot; there were several whom he recognised as having been employed by him before.

"Now then, Taka," Frank began, speaking in the local language. "The stuff's in the lorry, and we've got to get it sorted out into carrier-loads. Climb aboard and pass it down. And you fellows," he added, as Taka mounted and threw aside the crumpled sail, "take it from him and lay it out here on the ground."

In the level rays of the rising sun Frank sorted out the blanket-rolls and boxes of stores into loads of more or less equal weight, chatting meanwhile to Kent, who had strolled out in pyjamas to watch the preparations.

Presently Mansfield also emerged, and stood eyeing the array of packages. He had not seen them before, owing to the crumpled sail that had hidden them in the lorry, and they looked a meagre amount to him. Half the things he had expected to see were missing; he could not even see a tent. He remarked on the fact.

Frank, bending over his work, turned his head. But before he could reply Kent broke in:

"Tent? What the deuce do you want a tent for? All very well in the rains, but useless in the dry season. There are plenty of spreading trees to camp under—shade by day and keep the dew off your blankets at night." He gave a scornful snort. "Only Government officials and parasites o' that kind lug tents and camp furniture and foot-warmers into the bush. And they don't get far with them either—if you want to travel free from worry and with contented carriers you travel light."

Though all that was true enough Frank wished that it had been expressed differently. It was not so much Kent's words as his tone, and he saw Mansfield turn away with a frown and a shrug. Obviously Kent had not taken to his employer, possibly owing to his patent boredom the night before at his host's wordy reminiscences. Mansfield was hardly out of earshot before Frank's supposition was verified.

"I don't exactly envy you your ginger-headed friend," Kent commented. "I'll be seeing you back this way in a few days, chucking the whole business."

"Think so? I don't," Frank replied. "Though I've known him only a few days, I'm beginning to see there's better stuff in him than I thought. We'll cover a good deal of ground, and maybe run up against more than either of us reckons," he added, turning to follow Mansfield and soothe his injured feelings, "before we hit the return trail."

Frank little thought how strange those happenings were to be.

An hour later the party left, Frank and Mansfield tramping in front, and the laden carriers following in a chattering string behind. For the first few miles they travelled along a washed-out and abandoned track that led to a deserted trading-store, and on reaching it they halted at a pool nearby for their midday meal.

It was not a cheerful spot, for an aura of desolation and broken hopes brooded over it. The ruins of the dead trader's primitive buildings were crumbling under the attacks of white ants and the encroaching bush and creepers, and Frank was not sorry when it was time to push ahead along the narrow native path that wound its way onward through the endless ranks of trees.

Frank went to a good deal of trouble to plan each day's march so that it should be reasonably short, and at the same time bring them to water before camping; for he knew that it would take time for Mansfield's legs to harden to the work. His forethought bore fruit, for, not being unduly fatigued, Mansfield settled down to conditions that were entirely strange to him more quickly than the other had dared to hope.

It was the fourth day after leaving Kent's place. The two men were resting under a shady tree. On one side of them the carriers were squatting round a little cooking-fire and on the other, in the bed of a partially dry donga, a shallow pool glinted in the fretted sunlight that fell through the overhanging foliage.

"I think this must be about our jumping-off place, where the trail begins," Frank remarked, pushing back the tin plate from which he had been eating.

Mansfield, lying on his back, with his hands behind his head, sat up.

"You mean it was somewhere about here my cousin left the party?"

Frank nodded. "As near as I can make it out from the evidence I could gather, or rather from what Mr. Larkman gathered for me. The place where they slept the previous night is some miles ahead of us, and apparently Oglethorpe was found to be missing when they were abreast of Doma Mountain, which we passed this morning. This spot is about half-way between the two."

Mansfield glanced round at the encircling trees, some of them still shady like the one under which they sat, but the majority, with seasonal change, standing almost bare amid a litter of red-brown leaves. "It looks as if I'm up against more than I thought," he admitted— "especially after the lapse of over two years. A pretty cold scent, what?"

Frank laughed. "There's no scent at all; we don't even know whether he turned off this path to the right or the left. We've just got to start at zero and puzzle it out." He lifted his head and called towards the carriers' fire, "Taka, come here!"

The head native came up, and Frank went on, "You probably know this area better than I do. Are there any villages hereabout?"

Taka jerked up his head in the affirmative of the native. "Yes, master; Chigagi's lies over yonder." He waved his left hand. "About as far as a man may walk in an hour."

"What sort of a place is it? Large?" Frank queried.

"Chigagi's is a village of about twenty huts, and there

are some smaller ones near by. Chigagi is headman of all of them."

"Very good, we'll go there next," Frank replied. "You'd better get the loads together, for we'll shift in a few minutes."

"What did he say?" Mansfield asked as Taka turned away.

Frank translated. "We may or may not find out anything from these people," he went on, "but it's obviously our first port of call." He rose slowly to his feet, stretched himself, and picked up his rifle, which he had leaned against the tree-trunk behind him.

For half an hour they threaded their way through the trees, and then emerged on a belt of cultivated land from which the crops had long since been gathered. Judging by the scattered remains of maize and millet stalks lying about, Frank reckoned that the yield must have been poor that year. The ground proved difficult to walk across, for it was corrugated everywhere with hoed-up ridges, which the sun had baked to the hardness of iron; but presently they struck a little path. It widened to quite a track, and ascended a rise that was crowned by a group of huts whose thatched roofs, stained russet from weather and from countless cooking-fires, glowed redly against the background of the bush.

Frank selected a suitable spot not far from the village, and began in a leisurely fashion to superintend his men making camp. Mansfield was impatient for him to hunt up the headman and start questioning him, but Frank shook his head.

"I'm as keen as you are," he said, "but there's a right way and a wrong. It's his job to come to us, not ours to go to him. There's an etiquette in these matters, and he'd think us people of no account if we hurried over immediately on arrival, and we'd get nothing out of him."

Presently Frank noticed figures moving among the huts, and a little party approached the camp, Chigagi at their head. He was an old man with a wrinkled body inadequately clad in a skin loin-cloth and a string of beads. Native fashion, he squatted down on the edge of the camp and began to clap his hands softly together in greeting. His followers did the same.

Frank took no notice of him for a minute, and then spoke.

The old man replied, and added an apology for not bringing the usual small present of welcome—eggs or a bowl of meal. They were starving, he protested, for their crops had failed. Frank nodded, putting the information aside for future reference, and opened the question of what had brought Mansfield and himself to the spot.

Chigagi shook his white-woolled head. "We have not seen a white man for many moons; they never come here, never." Mumbling, he harked back to the matter of his own poor harvest, trailing on into a mournful description of the outlook ahead until the next crop could be reaped.

Frank turned to the younger men of Chigagi's retinue. Their answers were far more concise than the old man's rambling monotone, but the result was much the same. They were positive they had not seen anybody, alive or dead, who could possibly have been Oglethorpe; the only white men they ever saw was an occasional hunter, and now and then a police trooper on hut-tax patrol.

Frank dismissed the visitors and turned to Mansfield, who was awaiting impatiently the outcome of the interview.

"No luck—as yet," Frank reported. "But that doesn't necessarily mean that your cousin didn't come this way. You never know with these people; they may be afraid to speak for fear of being involved in some official inquiry. 'Least said soonest mended' is only too often the native's motto."

"But couldn't they be induced to speak? I'm quite willing to offer a good reward." His hand unconsciously moved towards the spot where, in civilisation, he had always carried his note-case.

Frank smiled. "Money's no good to these folk—where could they spend it? No, we've got to think of something better than that. These people are hungry. Our best line is to stop here a day or two and shoot a few antelope for them. There's plenty of game about. With their stomachs full of meat they'll feel far more inclined to talk."

CHAPTER THREE

THE FIRST CLUE

ON the following morning Frank set out, accompanied by a couple of the local savages who knew the likely places to find game. Mansfield remained resting in camp, for he was not too fit. As is so often the case with rather florid people unused to the tropical rays, his arms and neck and even his face were raw and peeling from sunburn. His skin would harden in a few days, but meanwhile Frank had advised him to take it easy.

In the early morning light Frank threaded his way between the trees. Though he felt sorry for Mansfield, he was glad to be without him, knowing the handicap of an inexperienced companion. He wanted meat, and wanted it quickly, and a glance at the ground marked with the spoor of many kind of game animals told him that the getting of it should not be difficult.

Twice there was a rush of something breaking away through the trees, but no chance of a shot. Presently they descended to the edge of an open *vlei*—a treeless depression from which the long, dry grass had already been burnt off. In the middle of it, grazing on the young green shoots that spring up after a fire, was a herd of eighteen or twenty sable antelope.

Frank sank to the ground and took a good look at the intervening country. A couple of big ant-heaps and a few scattered bushes would provide sufficient cover for stalking within reasonable range. Signing to the natives to wait, he made his way forward with bent knees and a crouching back.

His first shot was true, and a fine bull collapsed. The startled herd swung round, and paused for a moment before dashing away. Frank fired again, and dropped a second sable, whereupon the others galloped for the cover of the trees, leaving a drifting cloud of dust and ashes in their wake.

Frank went up to the beasts he had shot, where he was quickly joined by the delighted savages, who saw a gorgeous feast in prospect when the two sable, each the size of a donkey, were cut up and brought in. Frank felt he had made a good start, and a couple more days of hunting should provide the hungry villagers with a store of food, both fresh and dried, for future use. If the local people knew anything about Oglethorpe, he was confident it would not be long before their tongues were loosened.

The next day Frank spent in a similar fashion, while Mansfield continued to hang about the camp, nursing his sore arms and face. His sunburn was rapidly improving, but the same could not be said of his temper, and Frank wondered what was the matter. On the third morning, just as Frank was preparing to go out, things came to a head.

"How much longer are we going to hang about here?" Mansfield growled. "I didn't come here to sit about and be bored stiff. Where's the information you said you would get out of these black native blighters?"

"Expect to get hold of some soon," Frank replied cheerfully, hoping Mansfield would respond and look less glum. "I know it's a nuisance, but there it is."

"Oh, it's all right for you," Mansfield snarled back. "You're having a darned good time shooting. You should remember what you're here for, instead of amusing yourself at my expense."

Frank swung round and faced the other squarely. "If that's what you think, we part right here. I'm through with the whole business."

Mansfield realised that he had gone too far. His eyes dropped and he muttered an apology.

Frank was not one to keep up a quarrel. "All right, we'll say no more about it. Meanwhile, as you've pointed out, you're my employer, so you'd better give your orders. Got anything better to suggest?"

"No, I haven't," Mansfield admitted. "I expect you're on the right lines. I—er—" His voice trailed away.

Frank studied him critically for a moment. "Look here, old chap, what's the trouble? Something's wrong, I can see that."

"I suppose the bottom of it is that everything's strange, and I've nothing to do. You're away from the camp all day, and here I sit with only these natives, who don't speak a word I understand."

Frank nodded comprehendingly; he had once experienced the same lost feeling himself.

"That's easily remedied," he said. "Have a shot at learning the local language. It might be invaluable to you later—you never know. I'll give you a few key words, and you'll soon pick up the rest by context."

He saw Mansfield's face brighten. "Why, yes, that's an idea. Now I expect you want to be off. Sorry I was a bit of a beast just now," he added, holding out his hand.

"Oh, that's all right," Frank said as he grasped it cordially, and with a cheerful nod turned away for his morning prowl round.

Oddly enough, the brief friction with Mansfield made him feel more hopeful about the future than he had done from the start. Somehow it had cleared the air and brought more understanding between them. Frank realised that the blame had been partly his—he had not made sufficient allowance for everything being so strange and different from anything Mansfield had hitherto experienced. He would see that things went more smoothly in the future. Meanwhile, he must turn his thoughts to the matter in hand.

As Frank's usual natives were not with him that day, he picked up a man from one of the outlying villages, who would be able to guide the carriers later if anything had to be brought in.

Frank had not gone more than half a mile beyond the hamlet when he came on fresh buffalo spoor and drop-pings—the first he had seen in that area. As a quick examination showed that the animals could not have passed more than a few minutes before, he turned to follow up the trail.

It was not long before he caught up with the slowly moving herd. He could hear their feet crunching on the fallen leaves and the occasional low call of one of the cows to her calf. But the bush was dense, and except for the glimpse of some black flank, or the swing of a tail, he could see nothing of them. Cautiously he tried to get closer, expecting every moment that they would hear him or get a whiff of his scent.

At last his opportunity came. He had a brief but clear vision of the massive bulk of a bull passing across a gap. Frank's rifle went up, and he fired, and the unmistakable thud of the bullet striking flesh told him he had hit his target. The herd broke into a thunderous stampede and crashed away through the forest.

Frank and the native with him reached the spot, to find that the beast he had wounded had not fallen, but had gone off with the rest, leaving tell-tale crimson drops on the dead leaves to mark its passage. The two followed the blood spoor. Presently they saw that the animal had turned aside from the others—a sure sign of a serious hurt. The two followed steadily, Frank with his rifle ready for instant action and his eyes peering into the foliage ahead.

Meanwhile the wounded bull was doing the old trick of its species—circling round so as to cut its own trail. Close to where its feet and blood had so recently marked the ground it halted, and backed itself into a mass of dense cover, where its black bulk and widespread horns were almost invisible amid the deep shadows. Grimly it waited for its pursuers to pass.

The first that Frank knew of the buffalo's manouvre was a sudden crash behind him. He spun round to see the bull charging savagely out from its ambush a few yards away.

The terrified native who followed him was in the line of fire. Frank yelled to the man to jump aside. The native made a convulsive leap, caught his foot in a twining creeper, and fell flat on his face.

It was a matter for split-second decision. The charging bull was almost on top of them, and no shot would now stop it in time. Frank grabbed the fallen native by one arm, and with a quick heave jerked him almost from under the buffalo's pounding feet, the effort sending the two of them rolling together into a thorn-bush, while the beast thundered by within a yard, shaking the ground.

It took a moment or two for it to slow up and turn, and Frank seized the chance. He scrambled to his feet, and as the animal swung round to renew the attack he fired. The buffalo lurched, and collapsed with a slithering thud that sent up a whirl of dust and dead leaves.

Now that the excitement was over Frank realised it

had been a close thing. But such incidents are likely when hunting dangerous game, and there was nothing in it to make a fuss about. No doubt the native was grateful, but he would not know how to express it— which was not to be regretted from his rescuer's point of view.

Frank lighted his pipe, and after reminding his follower to take careful note of the spot, so that he could guide the carriers back to it to cut up the carcass, he turned his face towards the camp.

Presently the native, who was still trembling from his fright, spoke. "That was an evil beast indeed, master," he murmured.

"Sure thing," Frank replied over his shoulder, "However, if he'd got you, there's plenty more where you come from," he added with a grin. "It's white men like me who are scarce!"

"Yes, master; few of them come here." A pause. "You seek one of them, master—one who was here more than two dry seasons and two wet seasons ago?"

Frank turned sharply. "Ah! Do you know anything about him?"

"A little, a very little, master."

"Then why haven't you said so before? You know I've been asking every day at Chigagi's village."

"They know nothing, so could not tell. They never saw him. But I did. The master saved me from the buffalo, and though I have feared to speak I will do so now."

"Well?"

"As the master knows, I live at the little group of huts in the bush where I joined him this morning. There was a stranger, wearing the kind of clothes I have heard that white men wear in towns. He appeared out of the bush

As the buffalo swung round, he fired.

when I was squatting by my hut, carving a bowl. He demanded food, and when I was slow in bringing it he struck me with his fist and knocked me down. Then he went into my hut and took all I had; but after he had gone I found he had dropped a small metal box from his clothing. I kept it to use for snuff. See—I have it here."

He fumbled under his scanty loin-cloth and held out something in his hand.

Frank took it. It was, or had once been, a silver cigarette case.

"Why didn't you show me this before?" he asked, as he turned it over.

The man shuffled his feet awkwardly. Frank guessed his true reason: the fear of saying anything lest he should find himself involved in some unforeseen trouble or inquiry.

"Are you sure you found this as you say?" Frank went on. "You didn't find the white man lying dead in the bush, by any chance, and take it from his body?"

The other shook his head vigorously. "No man of my tribe would touch the corpse of one of another race, lest the spirit should haunt him. No, master, it was as I have said: he came and he went again, and he dropped the metal box in his haste and anger."

Frank felt convinced that the man was speaking the truth. He began to examine the case more closely. It was tarnished and dented, from over two years under a native's belt, but it had been originally an expensive article. He slanted it so as to catch the light, and his heart gave a jump. Though the engraving was blurred and rubbed, it bore Oglethorpe's name in Gothic script.

Frank raised his head. "I will keep this, and in exchange you shall have a fine transparent bottle for your snuff." He remembered a small glass bottle amongst his kit. "Also you shall have much buffalo meat for yourself. Now there's one other thing I want to know. You saw the man leave—which way did he go?"

Without hesitation the native raised his arm and pointed. Even after a lapse of years a native never forgets a direction, and can point as accurately as a compass. Frank took a quick glance at the position of the sun and the line of the outstretched arm and gave a grunt of satisfaction.

"Due north-east," he murmured, "as near as no matter. Now I think we're beginning to get hold of something at last."

Without more ado Frank made straight for the camp, and as he strode into it Mansfield read the look on his face. He sprang to his feet. "You've found out something?"

"I have. Let's have a drink first—hi, Taka, hurry up with that kettle!—and then I'll tell you." Frank rested his rifle against a tree and threw himself down on his bedding-roll.

As he drank the scalding tea that Taka had brought, Frank told Mansfield of his morning's adventure and its sequel. Finally he produced the cigarette case and passed it across.

Mansfield examined it. "Yes, it's his. Apart from the name engraved on it, I recognise the shape and design. Indeed I've had a cigarette from it before now, on the few occasions we happened to meet. That proves he was here, but I don't see it takes us a great deal farther."

"The native tells me he hurried off to the north-east, and I gather he covered the ground like a man who knows he has a long way to go."

"That so?" Mansfield gave a slight shrug. "I don't see that helps a lot—he may have jinked later in any direction."

"You don't see the significance? I do; and, what's more, it bears out your theory that his whole action after the plane crash was deliberate. North-east from where we sit is the shortest distance to the border of Portuguese territory—if you look at the map of Africa you'll see a projecting piece of it extending up the Zambezi Valley. The nearest point can't be more than fifty miles off."

"I never thought of that," Mansfield admitted, "but it's quite likely."

"More than likely—almost certain," Frank commented. "You tell me the British police were after him just then. Once over the frontier he'd be in country wilder even than this, where the Portuguese police would be unlikely to trouble him, even in the event of an extradition warrant, the question of which, of course, never arose."

Mansfield slapped his knee. "I believe you're right! He's there, I'll bet."

"Unless he's pushed on to the Portuguese settlements," Frank grinned, "and set up there as a bank manager or a missionary."

Mansfield laughed. "I wouldn't put even that past him. But I doubt it. Too risky. Someone would start getting curious, and then the fat would be in the fire. I know his limitations, and so does he. No, a nice quiet hide-out was what he was after."

the infant flames could assume full size the loads were hastily transferred to the widening patch of cooling ash. Men and baggage were safe upon a black island that every minute grew slowly larger.

Frank had time now to see how Mansfield was taking the situation. He found him dabbing at a long scratch from a thorn and gazing through the reek of their own little burn towards the enemy from which they had fled.

It was an awe-inspiring sight. As they roared onwards through the long, dry grass from which the travellers had so recently emerged, the flames were leaping thirty or forty feet into the air, throwing out volumes of black smoke that was streaked here and there with white steam as some damper patch was struck. Well in advance of them a bevy of black flycatchers turned and swooped, eagerly snapping at insects; while high overhead circled a pair of eagles, also watching for some escaping prey.

But the birds were not the only moving things to be seen, for the whole world was on the run. From the refuge of their burnt patch Frank and Mansfield saw a herd of eland—the largest of the antelopes—go by at a sharp trot. An old wart-hog boar and sow raced past, with snouts outstretched and tails erect, to be followed by three koodoo bulls, their horns laid back on their withers as they ran through the belt of trees. All around were hurrying feet and moving forms, each creature filled with one idea only: to escape from the death behind.

The flames were close now, and their crackling roar was deafening. Sparks fell in showers on the party, together with burning twigs as the edge of the trees was reached. Drawn by the upward rush of heated air, the little circle of protecting fire leaped up as if in greeting. The moving curtain of scarlet and orange reached the rim of the burn, and parted as if divided by an invisible hand. Sinking as the grass became shorter, it passed on either side, leaving in its wake a blackened world and a choking reek of drifting smoke.

The fire had passed, and in a few minutes it would be possible to continue the journey. It might be a dirty job, owing to the fine ash, but at least there would be no tangling grass. Coughing and wiping his streaming eyes, Frank turned to examine the loads and make sure the falling sparks had done no harm. It was then that he made an unpleasant discovery.

Three or four of the loads were composed of meal for the carriers, upon which Frank had been keeping a watchful eye. The amount was none too lavish, and, owing to finding Chigagi's people starving, he had not been able to supplement it on the journey. Two of the bags showed flatness instead of rounded contours, and white rivulets of leaking meal showed through the tears in their sides.

The explanation was simple. In their flight through the long grass the men who had carried them must have ripped them against projecting thorns, and, not noticing the wake of spilt meal they were leaving behind them, had stumbled blindly on.

As Frank looked down at the damage, Mansfield joined him and asked a question.

"It's unfortunate, to say the least of it," Frank replied. "Of course if the crops have been good in the Zambezi Valley below the escarpment it doesn't matter, for we can trade a fresh supply. Otherwise"—he shrugged his shoulders—"it will mean the carriers going hungry, and hungry carriers spell trouble. However, there's no point in climbing a fence till you come to it, as they say. Let's get started again; I want to reach a water-hole among the hills to-night, and if we pull out from there at the first light, we ought to reach the lip of the escarpment just after sunrise to-morrow."

Frank's calculation was right. The sun had just risen next morning when, winding through the hills, they saw ahead of them nothing but sky, and a few minutes later they had reached the edge of the escarpment itself.

Frank halted, and the carriers did the same, laying down their loads and exchanging snuff-boxes while they chattered. The wonderful view was beyond their appreciation; they were far more interested in the present snuff and the future prospect of finding a supply of native beer in the villages of the valley country.

But Frank's thoughts were very different. The spot gave him a strange uplifted feeling, as though he were standing midway between heaven and earth.

On either side the great bastions of the escarpment stretched away into the dim distance, buttressing up the plateau behind. Immediately in front, and a thousand feet below, projected the little foothills formed of debris that had fallen eons ago from the crest, and beyond them the ground levelled out into the widespread floor of the valley. The lines of its water-courses, mainly dry at that season of the year, but with water not far below their sandy surfaces, were picked out by thin ribbons of greener foliage against the russets and duns of the bush; while over them hung thin streaks of morning mist that the rising sun would soon dispel. Faint wisps of bluish wood-smoke marked the sites of none or two primitive native villages. Forty miles away, and invisible owing to the distance and the haze along the horizon, lay the great Zambezi River.

Frank turned his head sideways and looked at Mansfield, who had seated himself on a rock. He was sitting with his chin in his hands, gazing silently out at the view before him. Frank wondered what he was thinking about, and as he studied him he realised that Mansfield had changed considerably since the two had first met in Mr. Larkman's office. Not only did he appear less soft, which was to be expected after the hard life and harder marches he had already experienced, but he had lost the slightly petulant look that had been noticeable about his mouth. Frank felt he was watching an interesting transformation, rather like the slow development of a photographic negative.

Was Mansfield's sense of values changing, he wondered, and was he discovering that the world contained a great deal more of value than civilisation and money could offer?

As if in answer to Frank's ruminations, Mansfield slowly raised his head, tilted back his sun-helmet till a fringe of carroty hair appeared beneath the brim, and spoke.

"Makes you think—that," he said, indicating the vast panorama with a motion of his hand. "I've never been much of a religious bloke, but it gets me that way some-how. Sort of getting-down-to-brass-tacks feeling."

He paused for a minute, scratching his chin. The shadows of a couple of circling eagles passed across the face of the cliff below, and far in the distance came faintly the booming roar of a lion returning to its daylight lair.

"Money's useful," Mansfield went on, "but I'm begin-ning to wonder whether, after all, it's worth the sweat of running after it. Take this matter of Oglethorpe, now. He doesn't know he's due for a half-share of £40,000, or that the police are no longer looking for him at home; but would he be any better off if he did? He may be quite contented, wherever he is, while with the money he'd go slap back to his old rotten ways. And then there's myself.

I've enough to live on—would more than that be any great advantage?"

"Oh, I don't know," Frank replied, "but, then, I'm no judge. I've seldom had more than a couple of bob to clink together at any time, and I know I wouldn't mind a spot more to play around with. But this is your show. You must decide for yourself whether to carry on, or just let things go as they are."

Mansfield remained silent for a moment, and then threw up his head with a jerk.

"No, I'll be shot if I'll let that so-called charity concern get away with it! I can make better use of the money than leaving it to be wasted on what they call 'expenses' —in other words, putting nineteen shillings out of a pound in their pockets, and doling out the odd bob as a safeguard against prosecution. And as for Oglethorpe's share, his recent experiences may have taught him to pull up a bit. Anyway, we haven't found him yet, and the whole outcome depends on that." He rose abruptly to his feet. "Come on, let's be moving."

At a sign from Frank the carriers picked up their loads and balanced them again on their heads, and the party turned to negotiate the steep descent from the plateau to the low country.

It was a job needing care, for the drop was abrupt. It was a matter of a step at a time, for each foothold had to be sought and tested. In a long zig-zag the travellers descended. Now and then a cry of warning came from those behind as a stone dislodged itself under their groping feet, and those below pressed themselves close against the rock as the missile bounded past on its way to the tree-tops beneath. But at length all reached the bottom unharmed, and after a short pause to see that all the packs were secure, they struck out through the jumbled screes and foothills towards the main floor of the valley.

Frank and his companions found themselves moving in an entirely different world. For one thing, the temperature was considerably hotter, for when they had reached the level they were nearly three thousand feet lower than their camp of the night before. For another, the type of bush had altered completely.

Except near the water-courses, where huge timber and occasional palms shot up to the sky, the bush was not typically tropical—the trees were not tall, but what they lacked in height they made up in density. Much of the ground was covered with jungle so thick that penetration was possible only along chopped native paths or well-beaten game-tracks, while amid the tangle huge and ungainly baobabs—that monstrosity of the vegetable world—loomed up vast and grey, and threw grotesque shadows from their distorted limbs. Only in the belts of mopani forest was it possible to move independently of tracks, for the mopani, like the English beech, kills everything beneath it, and its tall black stems stand rank upon rank above a soil bare except for its own fallen leaves.

CHAPTER FIVE

IT was a typical village of the low country. Eight or ten huts, somewhat cleaner and tidier than those of the plateau natives, were perched above a narrow river bed, from which water could be obtained by digging a hole in the sand and letting it percolate through. On the other three sides dense bush closed it in, making it invisible until one was actually entering the clearing.

On the edge of this clearing Frank and Mansfield rested beneath a patch of shade, and some little distance away the carriers squatted round a tiny fire. They were not chattering in their usual manner, but talking in low tones, and presently one of the figures rose to its feet and advanced.

Frank looked up. "Well, Taka, what do you want? I didn't call you."

"No, master, but the others asked me—" He paused.

"Asked you what?" Frank spoke gruffly, for he had already noticed the sulky attitude that had appeared among the men.

"You do not give us our proper amount of meal, master, and we feel hungry."

"Is that my fault?" Frank retorted. "Go and grumble at those two who tore their bags and scattered the meal that day of the fire. If it hadn't been for their carelessness I shouldn't have been forced to reduce your ration."

"The long marches make us hungry. We want more meal, master," Taka persisted.

"And where the deuce am I to get it?" Frank demanded. "These people"—he indicated the huts of the village—"have none to spare. I wish they had. I'm hoping farther along to strike a place with a surplus."

Taka shuffled his feet nervously, but stood his ground.

"I'll try to shoot you a buck to-morrow," Frank went on. "That's the best I can do, and you know it. Now go and tell the others what I've said."

"But meat is only *chisara*"—a word best translated as "flavouring." "We want meal for porridge, good thick porridge to fill our stomachs."

Frank stuck out his chin. "Now look here, Taka, you stop talking rubbish. Meat's food, and good food, and you ought to be thankful to get it to supplement your meal ration. Chigagi's people were grateful enough for what I shot for them. Now get out, and if I have any more nonsense from you, there'll be trouble!"

Taka sulkily returned to his comrades, and Mansfield, who had already learned enough of the native language to gather the gist, asked a question.

"Though we may have had to cut their ration a bit," Frank replied, "I've a shrewd idea that it's all a put-up excuse. I've had carriers go short quite cheerfully before, knowing the circumstances. Besides, with plenty of meat they can live like fighting-cocks. No, the bottom of the trouble is something quite different. Down here these fellows are in a strange country and among a different tribe, and every march takes them deeper into it. They've got the wind up, and want us to go back."

"But they took on for the journey, didn't they?" Mansfield put in. "They raised no objection then."

"Probably they didn't realise how far we meant to go. I must say I thought better of Taka, and of some of the others, too, for that matter; but they're like a lot of sheep when they get an idea into their heads. However, we're going on, whether they like it or not," Frank added grimly, "so Mister Sulky Taka and his pals had better make up their minds to it."

Though Frank had spoken confidently of getting meat to make up the deficiency in the meal supply, the area through which they marched after leaving the village was not very favourable to success. They were moving diagonally across the floor of the valley, slanting north-east for the nearest point of the Portuguese border, and owing to the time of the year there was very little surface water. In consequence the game had mainly left for the vicinity of the Zambezi to the north or the escarpment to the south, and, to add to the difficulty, the bush was thick and tangled, and it was impossible to see more than a few yards in any direction.

But it was not entirely deserted, as spoor and droppings showed. It still held a few elephants and quite a number of rhino—both creatures with a wide range of movement. Frank knew the danger of a sudden encounter at close quarters, and tramped in the van with all his senses on the alert. Meanwhile Mansfield brought up the rear, to ensure that the carriers did not lag or tail out in a long string.

It was shortly after the midday halt that the encounter occurred. Close to the track a rhinoceros was sleeping in the heat of the day, its great body invisible amid a tangled thicket. Frank passed it, and the leading carriers did the same, and then a puff of wind brought the intruders' scent to the dozing monster.

With a snort and a violent crash of breaking wood it got to its feet and charged, its twin horns and wicked-looking head bursting through the screen of branches into the middle of the string of tramping men.

With wild yells of alarm the natives bolted in panic, each leaping for the nearest tree up which he could scramble, oblivious of what happened to the load he had been carrying. Frank, at the head of the line, spun round to see nothing but a litter of scattered bundles and a twinkle of black legs, with the grey bulk of the rhino filling the centre of the picture.

The beast was more startled than vindictive. By luck its pounding feet missed treading on any of the abandoned packages, and the next moment it had crashed into the trees on the other side of the path, and the sound of its violent passing slowly died away in the distance.

No material harm was done, but the moral effect remained. Taka and his companions were already in a surly mood, and the incident did not improve matters. They felt more than ever convinced that each step was leading them farther into unknown dangers and discomforts, and though the sounds of the rhino's departure had long since ceased, Frank had to speak sharply before he got them down from their perches and they picked up their loads once more.

A mile or so ahead the bush became less dense, for the tangle gave place to more open mopani forest. Frank felt more hopeful here of getting a shot at something for meat, and he was not disappointed. He caught a glimpse of the pale grey coat and spiral horns of a koodoo between the trunks, and fired.

The buck jumped convulsively, but did not fall. At a tucked-up run it made off.

Frank jerked out the empty case and slipped in another cartridge from the magazine. "Mansfield!" he called.

"Hallo!" Mansfield came hastening up from the rear. "Did you get it?"

"No, but it's hard hit. I must follow—no time to waste. But look here. If we separate I'll probably be unable to find you again. Will you take charge and hustle the carriers along after me, trying to keep me in sight? The beast's not likely to go far, and then we shall all be together when it comes to cutting up the meat."

"That's O.K.; you carry on," Mansfield replied. "If we lose sight of you, at least we'll hear your finishing shot. If you come on it dead you'd better fire a shot anyway, to guide us."

"Yes, I will." Frank hurried off on the trail of the wounded beast, leaving the natives, who had already brightened slightly at the prospect of meat, to follow under Mansfield's charge.

Once or twice Frank caught a glimpse of his quarry, losing sight of it again before he could get in another shot. Presently above the surrounding tree-tops he saw ahead of him the crest of a rocky ridge, part of a small group of hills that islanded the level ground. The trail of the wounded beast led straight towards them. It was making for the sanctuary of the tangled kloofs and slopes, for koodoo, though seen in most parts, are essentially hill-dwellers.

Frank found himself entering a ravine, fairly wide at the mouth, but narrowing and sloping upwards as he progressed. Thicker bush closed around him, the gnarled roots of the trees twisting fantastically among the rocks in their search for sustenance between them. The fleshy, cactus stems of huge euphorbias rose above him like bunches of bright green pipes from some cathedral organ, while on the flanking cliffs splashes of scarlet flowers amid a mass of pointed spikes showed where aloes clung to their foothold.

Guided by the blood-drops on the stones, Frank came suddenly on a little open space, a small grassy bay let in the side of the valley. In the middle of it lay something grey and still—the koodoo had reached the end of its strength and had dropped.

He approached the dead beast and stood over it, panting slightly from his scramble. He had secured his meat, but the diversion from the path which the party had been following had taken time, and haste would be needed if the beast were to be cut up and the intended halting-place reached before darkness fell. The sun was already near the horizon. Now, if only there were water handy, he ruminated, camp could be made on the spot and the job done in a leisurely fashion.

Those hills were quite a likely place. Frank raised his head and sniffed. Surely he could *smell* water? It was not lower down the valley, so it must be higher up.

He climbed a few steps farther up the narrowing ravine. He lifted himself over a shelf of boulders, and then he saw it—a glassy and sombre-looking pool encircled by black rock over which grotesque euphorbias and gnarled trees with leaves of a deep metallic green stood like sentinels. The problem was solved, and the work of securing the supply could be done without haste.

Frank returned to where the dead beast lay, and then suddenly recollected that he had fired no signalling shot. Those behind must be wondering where he was. He raised his rifle, and the echoes of the report rolled and boomed about him, while from somewhere high up on the overshadowing cliffs came the gruff and challenging bark of a startled baboon. Half a minute later the sharp crack of Mansfield's answer rang out and presently he heard Mansfield's distant shout. Frank replied, and at length came the rattle of dislodged stones as the party ascended the ravine.

"So you got it?" said Mansfield as he stepped into the little clearing and caught sight of the dead koodoo. "That's a good thing. Now perhaps these black chaps'll cheer up. My goodness, but I've had quite a job to hustle 'em along up here after hearing your signal shot— you'd have thought they'd only one leg apiece by the way they moved. Rum spot this," he added, glancing up at the cliffs and the trees sprouting between the encircling rocks.

"There's water here," Frank replied, jerking his head up the ravine. "Quite a decent-sized pool that looks as if it were fed by some underground spring. The overflow must sink away, for there's no sign of water lower down. Instead of pushing on as we'd meant to do, I'm for stopping here the night. It's nearly sunset now."

"Good enough. I'm agreeable. After the rhino business a few miles back, I'm not eager to push on in the dark. I say," he added as his glance fell on the natives, "the sight of meat seems to have woken up those blokes at last. You'd think time was worth a pound a minute by the way they're smacking into it."

It was true. Taka and his companions had put down their loads, and were setting to work at the job of skinning and cutting up with desperate haste. There was none of the cheerful chatter of natives engaged in a congenial task; they were putting every ounce of energy into the matter in hand.

"All right, there, go easy," Frank said, as one of them started to tear off the skin without pausing to sever the ligaments that held it to the flesh. "You can take your time, for I'm intending to make camp here for the night."

If he had exploded a bomb under their noses they could not have looked more startled and alarmed.

"Master, we cannot stay here," Taka broke out; "we must get back to the path and hasten on to the next water."

Frank raised his eyebrows. "Why? There's good water yonder—I've seen it. So we'll stop here instead."

"Master, no! This is a fearsome place, and no man can camp here."

"But why not?"

"It is a fearsome spot," Taka repeated. "It is full of magic and haunted by the spirits of the dead!"

Remembering Taka's recent attitude, Frank felt his temper rising, but he kept it under control. "What makes you say that?" he asked.

Taka threw out his hands expressively. "Every man knows it. We have heard it spoken of in the villages we have passed through, and we have even heard tell of this place far away in our own homes. None but those who have the magic power and who can control the spirits can linger here and live."

"What's the trouble?" Mansfield asked, for Taka's agitated utterances were too rapid for him to follow with his limited knowledge of the language.

"He says the place is taboo," Frank explained. "Probably these hills are the private preserve, fetish-grove, or whatever you like to call it, of some old witch-doctor with a big local reputation, who has metaphorically put up a 'Trespassers-keep-out' notice."

"That so?" Mansfield commented. "Pity he doesn't show up right now," he added flippantly, "and we'd get him to amuse us by performing some of his conjuring tricks. Meanwhile, what are you going to do about it?"

Normally Frank would have given way, for he was always careful not to offend native susceptibilities. But in the present case he was tired, and his temper was already frayed by the past behaviour of Taka and his companions.

"Don't let me have any more of your infernal nonsense!" he broke out. "I'm fed up to the back teeth with the lot of you! Half of you get on with that cutting-up job, and the rest of you go and collect firewood and make camp. Do you hear what I say? Get busy, then! What are you waiting for? My oath, if you look at me again like that, Taka, I'll give you something real to complain about!"

The orders were obeyed, the natives separating for their different tasks. At first there was a good deal of muttering, too low for Frank to catch, but presently this ceased, and the men began to move about more briskly. As Frank watched them he felt that his little outburst of temper had been a good thing; there are times when a man must put his foot down and show who is boss, and for some time Taka and his friends had been asking for it. Now perhaps they had seen that a discontented attitude didn't pay, and would resume their normal cheerfulness.

The last rays of the sun ceased to gild the tops of the cliffs above, and darkness gathered in the ravine. The natives had brought in a plentiful supply of dead wood, and the flickering light of the camp-fires reflected redly on the surrounding trees and rocks, picking them out sharply against the blackness beyond. Overhead, in the narrow ribbon of blue-black sky above the ravine, the stars came out one by one.

Frank and Mansfield ate their evening meal and presently sought their blankets. For a while Frank lay awake, idly listening to the night noises of the bush and thinking over the events of the day. At length he turned on to his side and settled himself to sleep.

Frank always woke early—a habit born of the need for early starts to avoid marching in the heat of the day. The unmistakable scent of dawn was in the air and, though darkness still reigned in the ravine, a hint of pale primrose was beginning to tint the star-strewn sky above. He lifted his head and noticed that the camp-fires had been carelessly allowed to die down, and were little more than glowing ashes.

"Hey! Taka!" he called. "Stir those fires, and shove on the kettle at the same time."

There was no reply. Frank sat up and shouted again, while Mansfield, roused by his voice, also stirred. There was no reply or sound of movement.

With a growl Frank rose and thrust his feet into his unlaced boots. He crossed to where the carriers had been lying, and halted with a sudden exclamation.

In the growing light of the dawn he could see the flattened pads of dry grass that had been strewn beneath the blankets, but there was no sign of either the blankets or their owners. While he and Mansfield slept every native had silently rolled up his scanty kit and deserted.

CHAPTER SIX

"ANYTHING the matter?" came Mansfield's voice from where he lay.

"I should jolly well think there is something the matter!" Frank retorted. "The carriers have hopped it —the whole lot of them."

It was Mansfield's turn to scramble to his feet and cross over. "Dirty dogs!" he commented. "Pinched what they can and done a midnight flit, have they?"

At the words Frank looked more closely round the deserted camp. Their own stores had been lying beside where the white men had slept and were intact, but the small remaining amount of native meal and a good deal of the koodoo meat had vanished. Though the deserters had left silently and in haste, they had taken thought for the morrow.

"What's the next move?" Mansfield continued. "I suppose we'll have to chase them and bring them back."

Frank shook his head. "Useless," he replied. "Even if we caught up with them we'd never get them; at the first glimpse of us they'd scatter and dive into the bush. No, they're finished with so far as we're concerned."

"I guess you're right—we'll have to think up some-thing else." Mansfield picked up the kettle and placed it on the glowing ashes. "Maybe we'll think better after a cup of tea; I don't know how you feel about it."

Frank realised the wisdom of the suggestion, though

Mansfield's calm way of taking the situation surprised him. He had expected much more fuss to be made—certainly Mansfield was getting tougher in every way. But no doubt he had not yet fully comprehended the problem before them.

They drank their tea, while the sky turned from primrose to pink and from pink to blue and the sun's first gleams touched the crests high above.

"That's better," said Mansfield as he put down his cup. "Now what are we going to do about this business?"

"There are two courses open to us," Frank replied. "One is to rake up more carriers from somewhere, and the other is to load ourselves up with what we can in the way of food, abandon the rest, and try to get back to civilisation."

"I don't cotton to the going-back idea—I might have done once, but that's ancient history. And the prospect of turning myself into a pack-mule and leaving all this stuff to rot doesn't appeal to me any, I can tell you. It's the first suggestion for me. Where are we going to look for them—back at the village we left yesterday morning?"

Frank shook his head. "Too small; there wouldn't be more than two or three able-bodied men there at the outside. Besides, our late carriers have gone that way and no doubt left a tale behind them that would dish all our chances. No, we must find a fresh village and a larger one."

"Then let's go and hunt for it. Have something to eat first, and then you go one way and I another."

"No, we'd better keep together. Meanwhile there's this stuff." Frank looked down at the loads containing their stores. "We ought to find a safer place to park it if we're going to be absent all day. If you'll have a shot at cooking something to eat, I'll have a scout round."

While Mansfield stirred up one of the fires Frank shouldered his rifle and moved up the ravine. He climbed the shelf of rock and reached the edge of the pool behind it.

In the bright morning light he had not expected the pool to have the same oddly sombre look that he had noticed on the previous evening, especially considering the vivid colours of the vegetation that grew between the boulders. Frank guessed that the water must be deep, for though it was clear he could see no bottom, and not a ripple disturbed its surface. On one side a cliff rose almost sheer above it, but the other offered a way past. Slowly Frank skirted the pool, stepping from one slippery rock to another, and wishing he had boots with rubber soles.

And then he saw it. Behind the pallid trunk of a tree whose roots sprawled over the black rocks like the knotted fingers of an old man's hand there was a dark opening in the hillside. Frank scrambled across for a closer view.

It was less of a cave than an alcove, high enough to stand up in, and penetrating inwards only a dozen feet, but it seemed exactly the place he wanted. The floor was dry, and the roof would protect the foodstuffs from the noonday sun. Moreover, it offered a good sleeping-place for the following night in case the search for carriers was unsuccessful, for the three solid walls and a fire across the entrance would ensure a rest undisturbed by any prowling wild beast.

Frank returned to where he had left Mansfield and told him of his discovery. Having eaten the food that had been prepared, they transferred their stores and blankets to the cavity—a job needing several journeys over the slippery rocks that bordered the pool. This done, they picked up their rifles and descended to the level ground to search for a village.

All day they wandered through the bush, listening for any sounds of wood-chopping or human voices, and keeping a sharp lookout for any path marked with the spoor of native feet. But luck was against them: the immediate vicinity of the group of hills seemed entirely uninhabited. Towards sunset, tired and hungry, they returned to the ravine and the little cave.

"Better luck to-morrow," Frank commented as they entered. "What we must do is to climb to the top of one of these hills first thing and look out for a wisp of smoke. It shows for miles at dawn, when the air is still; far better than ploughing about the bush on chance."

It was not difficult to collect a supply of fuel, for there was any amount of dead wood lying about the ravine, and it was not long before they had a cheerful fire burning at the entrance. As darkness fell the bright flames lit up the interior of the little cave, and by their ruddy glow Frank and Mansfield made the place comfortable, arranging their blankets and stores and preparing their evening food.

Presently, as they rested on their blankets, smoking, a series of heart-rending shrieks rang out suddenly from the darkness. Mansfield sat up with a jerk.

"What on earth's that?" he muttered.

Frank grinned. "It's not those 'evil spirits' that Taka talked so glibly about. By the sound, I should say a leopard has got his dinner. Yes," he went on, as the screams ceased suddenly, to be followed by a volley of hoarse barks, "he's got a baboon, and the others are putting in their protest from the safety of the higher rocks." Then as the noise lessened he added, "They've decided to shift now to a less dangerous locality, leaving that leopard to finish its feed in peace. And now that's all over, what about turning in and getting a good night's sleep?" Frank ended, knocking out his pipe.

His expectation of a restful night, however, was not to be fulfilled. He had been dozing only a short while when he found himself once more awake. He had a peculiar feeling that there was something outside the cave— something that watched and waited just beyond the rosy circle of the firelight. He assured himself that it was only some prowling beast of the night, and therefore harmless, for the flickering flames would keep any wild creature at bay. He tried to settle down to sleep again, but the feeling of watching eyes persisted.

He sat up, wondering what it could be. As if in reply to his movement he heard a laugh, but it was not an ordinary laugh. Not only did it seem to come from the very fire itself, but there was no human ring about it. It was altogether horrible, as if it had come from the lips of some grotesque satyr of the kind drawn by medieval monkish artists.

Frank heard Mansfield stir also, and his mumbled question, "What the deuce was that?"

"A hyena probably," Frank replied, though he knew well enough that though these beasts make very weird noises, the sound he had heard was no hyena's chuckle. There was something oddly uncanny about it, especially the way it had seemed to come from the heart of the fire. But of course it couldn't have done so; that must have been some peculiar freak of acoustics caused by the shape of the cavity and the ravine outside.

He lay back, but the feeling of being watched persisted. Presently he got to his feet and picked up the rifle that lay beside his blankets. Skirting the fire, he reached the mouth of the cave and looked out into the darkness.

There was nothing to be seen. He returned to fetch an electric torch from amongst his kit. If any creature were lurking in the vicinity its eyes would reflect the bright beam. But no lambent orbs gleamed as he flashed it round; it illumined only the black rocks and twisted vegetation and the steel-smooth surface of the sombre pool.

He was about to turn away when he thought he heard something rustle amongst the undergrowth to the left. He swung round the beam, but could see nothing. "Only some jackal," he said to himself, but at the same time it had given him an uncomfortable start. "Here, you clear off, whatever you are!" he ejaculated, and raising his rifle fired a couple of shots into the darkness.

The echoes of the reports boomed and rolled along the ravine. "Did you see anything? Did you hit it?" came Mansfield's voice.

"No, I just banged off. That ought to shift anything that's lurking—"

Luckily for Frank he had stepped inside the entrance as he spoke, for the next moment, with a tearing noise, a loose boulder slipped from the hillside above and fell with a splintering crash just where he had been standing. It might have been caused by the reverberation, or the panic flight of some startled baboons, but the coincidence was anything but a pleasant one.

Frank darted outside and flashed his torch upwards. There was absolutely nothing to be seen. Puzzled, he rejoined Mansfield inside the cave, and as he did so, apparently from the rocky roof immediately above their heads, came a derisive and satanic laugh.

Frank felt his hair begin to bristle, and cold shivers ran down his back. Taka's tale of the ravine being the haunt of evil spirits came back to him with a rush. He tried to thrust it aside, but he had been long enough in Africa to know that, despite the rapid spread of settlement, it is still a land where strange and unaccountable things do occur. After the shocks of the last few minutes that sound, coming from where no material creature could possibly be, took the stiffening right out of him.

He glanced at Mansfield, who replied with a sickly grin. For a moment or two they looked at one another in silence.

It was Mansfield who pulled himself together first.

"There seems a lot of funny business going on," he said, "enough to make anybody bolt like a scared cat. I'd like to know who's playing this jiggery-pokery. It may be good enough to keep the local natives off, and make those carriers of ours hop it, but it won't scare us. Supernatural my foot! I'd like to catch the blighter who's trying it on."

He glared round angrily, his face redder than usual and his hair matching the firelight—and as if in answer a groan and a gabble of meaningless words came from behind one of the boxes of stores.

Frank, braced by Mansfield's matter-of-fact words and with his nerves once more under control, sprang towards it. There was nothing whatever behind the box except the dry and sandy floor of the cave.

It was the most uncanny business he had ever struck.

There was no further sleep for either of them. There would be long periods of silence, and thinking that the unexplained phenomena had ceased altogether, they would take to their blankets once more; but immediately the whispers, wails, and chuckles of demon laughter would sound again from some quite impossible spot, banishing all chance of repose. Frank spent the rest of the night sitting moodily with his rifle across his knees, determined that if anything, human or otherwise, appeared, he would try a soft-nosed bullet on it; while Mansfield occupied himself with a pack of patience cards and swore savagely in reply to each fresh manifestation.

Dawn came at last, filtering pale and wan into the ravine.

In a thoroughly disgruntled mood the two stepped out into the half-light. Except that the colour had not yet emerged from the night, the ravine seemed the same as it had done before. Casting quick glances around them, they advanced towards the upper end of the pool that lay like a dark mirror beneath the overhang of the opposite cliff. Suddenly from high above came a sound, and, looking up sharply, they saw that a loose boulder had slipped from its bed and was hurtling down towards them.

They leaped back just in time. The rock struck almost at their feet and shattered, one of the pieces hitting Frank so that he staggered and fell. It was the second time that he had barely missed death from the same cause. As he regained his feet Mansfield gave a cry: "There's someone up there!"

Mansfield whipped up the rifle he carried and fired. He was nothing in the way of a shot, and he missed by a couple of yards, but the smack of the striking bullet had its effect. The crouching figure of a native began to scramble hastily away along the brow of the overhanging cliff. The next moment the man's foot slipped, and with a cry and an ineffectual clutch at the rocks, he dropped with a prodigious splash straight into the pool.

He came to the surface, struggling feebly and making no attempt to gain the shore. Frank guessed that he must have been knocked out by the concussion of striking the water from a height, and that if something were not done

The man's foot slipped and, with a cry, he dropped...

quickly he would drown. He thrust his rifle into Mansfield's hands and kicked off his boots.

Mansfield saw Frank's intention. "Good man," he exclaimed; "fish the beggar out, and then we may get to the bottom of all the hokey-pokey. I'd come and give you a hand if I could, but I can't swim and—"

His words were cut off abruptly by the splash of Frank launching himself into the pool.

As Frank had already concluded, the water was deep and unusually cold. He struck out for where the drowning man floundered, thankful that he looked too knocked out to start clutching at him. He got his grip and turned to swim back, towing the native behind him. Splashing and blowing, Frank reached the brink, and with Mansfield's help hauled his prize clear of the water.

CHAPTER SEVEN

THE light was stronger now, and they could see something of the native they had pulled from the water.

He was a middle-aged man, wrapped in a sodden cotton cloth. His face was less negroid and bore a look of greater intelligence than the average; his hands were long and slender, and tipped with filbert-shaped nails. Frank had a shrewd idea that he was no less a person than the much-feared witch-doctor himself, for he had already had it brought home to him that no ordinary native dared venture into the hills.

The man stirred and opened his eyes: dark as night they were, with an odd impression of innumerable reflecting facets rather than a smooth eyeball. He spat out a mouthful of water and glared resentfully at the two white men.

"So you've come to life again?" Frank remarked in the native tongue. "Well, who are you, and what do you mean by trying to kill us with that boulder?"

"I am Kalubi, the familiar of the spirits," came the proud retort. "This place is holy to them, and no common man may violate their sanctuary."

Frank nodded. His guess about identity had been correct. "I see. So the boulder you dislodged was your way of hinting we weren't wanted. A second hint," he added, remembering the previous one that had just missed him at the mouth of the cave.

"To those who anger the spirits death always comes," Kalubi replied oracularly.

Mansfield, who had been standing by trying to gather the gist of the discourse, put in a word here.

"Ask him about those noises in the night. Tell him we want to know how he managed to put all that spooky stuff across us."

Frank did so.

"What you heard were the voices of the spirits, floating invisible in the air and angry with the intruders into their domain," came the haughty answer.

Frank translated, and Mansfield broke into a guffaw of laughter. "Sez you!" he sneered; "what does he take us for?"

The words were in English and Kalubi did not understand them, but he sensed the gist, and the derisive laughter stung him to the quick.

His eyes flashed. "It is only fools who believe in what they can see and nothing else. There are spirits everywhere, all around us—in the earth, in the air, in the water. Men such as me, with the inner knowledge, have only to call and they will answer."

He threw back his head and looked upwards, saying something in an unknown tongue. Almost immediately, from the very apex of a spiky euphorbia tree whose fluted columns towered above them, came a reply, followed by the same derisive laugh that had already become familiar to Frank and Mansfield.

In a flash Frank tumbled to the explanation of the weird noises during the previous night, and he felt like kicking himself for not thinking of it before. He had often heard that the main weapon in the armoury of the witch-doctor was ventriloquism—the art of being able to throw a voice without moving the lips, so that the sound should appear to come from any point the speaker should select. Indeed, he remembered that it is a carefully guarded secret among the fraternity, passed down from one generation to another, and a man who cannot master it can never qualify, for without its awe-inspiring effects on the simple native mind half a witch-doctor's power would vanish. Kalubi had been lurking outside the cave during the darkness, doing his best to make those inside bolt in panic from the vicinity.

He glanced at Mansfield, upon whose face, startled at first, was also dawning a look of comprehension.

"He could get a guinea an hour as an entertainer at a Christmas party," Mansfield grinned. "Tell him that in the white man's country that sort of thing is done to amuse the kids."

Frank did so, though not quite as crudely, for despite his murderous attempts in the way of dislodging boulders and his soaked and clinging wrapper, Kalubi had a certain dignity that evoked respect.

He was by no means disconcerted by the attitude of his captors. He merely took a different line, and in the tone of a householder who has caught a suspicious character lurking in his back garden, demanded to know why they had trespassed on his private preserve.

Frank realised that the man seemed genuinely upset about it, and he replied with some patience. He spoke of the pursuit of the wounded koodoo and its ending, of the decision to make camp on the spot where it fell, and of the desertion of the carriers during the night, which had forced them to remain instead of continuing their journey. At the end of the recital Kalubi's resentful expression cleared; he saw that the intruders had been the victims of circumstance rather than deliberate trespassers.

S   C

Meanwhile Mansfield had been fidgeting impatiently during Frank's explanation, feeling that in the light of recent events Kalubi was being treated with too much consideration. He put in a word.

"If he reckons he's so clever, he'd better produce some carriers for us out of a hat, like a conjurer."

Putting it somewhat differently, Frank passed on the suggestion.

"I have only to say the word and they will come, ready and willing to carry your loads," Kalubi replied blandly. "Why should I not do so? You saved me from the water when death came close to me, and I see now that you are good men and that your lingering here on for-bidden ground was by chance. You are not like that other white man who came here, many moons ago—ah! he was evil indeed."

Kalubi frowned at the memory of a past grievance and went on: "From my hut yonder"—he motioned with his hand, indicating somewhere up the ravine and round the next curve—"I heard him coming, moving as heavily as an angry buffalo. He stopped to drink at this pool, and I hoped he was going away, but he came on and saw my dwelling. He advanced, breathing heavily, and spoke roughly in the white man's tongue. When he saw I did not understand he pushed me roughly aside. He entered my hut and stole my food and other things, and when I called down upon him the curse of the unseen he kicked me twice with his foot—me, the high priest of the spirits!"

The similarity of the tale to that which he had heard from the native near Chigagi's village, when the cigarette case had been produced, made Frank's thoughts jump immediately to Oglethorpe.

"How long ago was this?" he asked sharply.

Kalubi pondered for a moment. "Many moons," he said at length, "for twice have the rains fallen and twice have the streams dried up upon the flats."

Frank turned to Mansfield and, in case he had not caught it all, gave a rapid summary. "It's more than probable the fellow was Oglethorpe," he added. "The dates fit. We're not at fault; we've held pretty accurately to your cousin's trail."

"It is no doubt the man we are following," Frank went on to Kalubi. "Which way did he go after leaving here?"

The native's eyes brightened. "You are not seeking such a one from friendship, so you must be doing so from hate. He has insulted and injured you also, and you mean to slay him with your guns? That is good, ah! But much time has passed, and maybe you will not find him, for the curse of the unseen is swifter than the pursuit of man. Which way did he go? I did not see, for his violence forced me to flee away among the rocks. But I can ask." He rose to his feet. "Come, I can trust you, and it is needful to go to my dwelling."

The two followed the witch-doctor. Frank was not sorry to be moving, for, though the morning breeze was rapidly drying his shirt and shorts that the plunge into the pool had soaked, the process of evaporation was chilly and the hot sunlight had not yet penetrated the ravine.

Moving upwards, they rounded a slight curve and saw a little clearing not unlike that on which they had camped on the night when the carriers deserted. In the middle of it stood a neatly thatched hut, surrounded by a fence of upright poles.

They passed inside. From beside the smoothly plastered wall of the hut Kalubi brought forward a couple of quaintly shaped wooden stools, and signed to his guests to be seated. He then pulled aside the wicker door of the little dwelling and vanished from sight.

"What's he up to now?" Mansfield asked as he gingerly lowered himself on to the stool. "Gone to fetch us a drink?"

Frank spread out his legs to keep his balance, and grinned. "Gone to fetch the tools of his trade, more likely, or else change his wet wrapper. I don't blame him either," he added, twitching his shoulders under his damp shirt; "thank goodness the sun will be over the brow of the hills before long, and it will be warmer then."

A moment later Kalubi reappeared, still in the same garment, which no doubt was his only one. He carried a skin bag in his hand, and squatting down in front of the white men he emptied out the contents on the ground before them.

It was a mixed collection. There were cast snake-skins, a dried paw of a monkey, the skull of a stillborn baby, and sundry similar objects. There were also a number of tablets of curiously carved wood, such as those of his calling use for the purposes of divination.

The native picked up the tablets, shook them together like dice in his two hands, and let them drop in front of his squatting figure. For a moment he studied the way they had fallen, shook his head slightly, and picked them up again. The second throw was also barren, but the third seemed more satisfactory, while the fourth and fifth confirmed that result.

"When he left here, the evil man went—so!" Kalubi stretched out an arm and pointed. The direction he indicated was that which Frank and Mansfield had been steadily following, and it confirmed the supposition they had already formed.

Mansfield, however, was not unduly impressed. "It's probably just a lucky guess," he commented, "for he knows we can't check up on him. And how could he really tell anything from those gadgets of his? Besides, we don't even know for certain that the bloke who came here was Oglethorpe. Ask him to tell us what he was like, and see if I can recognise the description."

Kalubi shook his head. "He was a white man, that is all I can say. To me white men all look alike."

Frank remembered hearing the same remark made once by a travelling friend about the Chinese. That line did not look a very hopeful one. He was about to speak again when the witch-doctor went on:

"I cannot describe him, but I can show him to you."

He retired to the hut, and came out with an earthenware bowl filled to the brim with water. He placed it on the ground. For a minute he remained motionless, peering intently at the two seated men, and once more Frank noticed the strangely faceted look about the eyes. They seemed to glitter with a light of their own. Then Kalubi made a gesture towards the bowl.

"Look into the water and you will see the man."

Both Frank and Mansfield leaned forward. Frank could see nothing at all but the reflection of the sky above, but Mansfield gave a violent start and jerked back his head.

"Did you see anything?" Frank asked.

"I did, and it gave me a bit of a jar," came the reply. "I saw my cousin's face—no doubt about it. I recognised him instantly. How the deuce was that done, eh?"

"These chaps are no slouches when it comes to hypnotism," Frank commented. "What you saw reflected in the water was the image stored up in your subconscious brain. And that explains why I saw nothing: having never set eyes on the fellow, there was no memory of him to be reflected."

Mansfield turned a pair of puzzled and slightly scared eyes towards Frank.

"That may be so in some cases, but it wasn't in this. What I saw wasn't at all what I remember of Oglethorpe. He was always spick and span and well-turned-out. But the face I saw in the water was dirty and unshaven, and there was a long scratch across his cheek."

Frank whistled. "Just as he would have been when he passed through here. Our friend made you see what was in *his* brain, then."

Meanwhile Kalubi was smiling sardonically. "Are the white men satisfied now?"

"Sure thing," Mansfield gulped. "Tell him to pack up. I've seen enough to last me for a while. If he goes on," he added with a feeble attempt at a joke, "I might find myself seeing my Aunt Caroline, and that would about put the lid on it."

"There's one more thing," Frank put to Kalubi, remembering the whole crux of their quest; "is the man alive now?"

The witch-doctor bowed his head between his knees and sat rigid for a few minutes. Then he raised his face and spoke.

"I have asked, but I cannot answer, for the spirits speak only of the spirit, and the earthly form is nothing. Life and death are but changes; he may still walk the earth as a man, or he may be wearing the form of some beast of the forest or a snake moving through the grass— a fitting fate for one who has offended the unseen and struck its minister with his foot!"

Kalubi stood up suddenly and bundled his treasures

back into their skin bag. "You need men to go with you on your journey?"

"Yes, we do," Frank replied, and Mansfield nodded agreement, adding that he hoped they would be real ones. Clearly what he had just seen in the bowl of water had shaken his former scornful attitude.

Frank made a rapid calculation of the depleted loads. Five or six carriers would be ample for them, but there was one snag. Owing to Taka and his mates going off with the remaining supply, he had no meal to feed them.

He pointed this out to Kalubi, who replied that they would find their own. "I will tell them so," he added, "and before the shadows have moved the breadth of a man's finger they will be starting hither."

"What's he mean by that?" Mansfield muttered. "The nearest villages must be hours away, for, as we know already, there are none near these hills. By the way he speaks you'd think he was going to ring 'em up on the phone!"

"I think I know," Frank answered. "Native telegraph. You'll see in a minute."

Meanwhile Kalubi had picked up a small drum, tucked it under his arm, and left the enclosure. He scrambled a little way up the adjacent cliff and seated himself at the foot of a vertical slab of rock, putting the drum between his knees.

Thud, thud, thud-thud, thud! The notes of the drum, not loud, but oddly penetrating, rolled down the ravine. There was a pause, while the performer listened intently for a reply; then the drum took up the tale once more, sending its message in the ancient code that Africa knew thousands of years before Europe thought of broadcasting.

"Do you mean to say that a village miles away can hear that?" said Mansfield, amazed.

"Yes, and answer too. Oh, I know—we can't hear the distant reply, for we're in the wrong place. But he can up there, with the cliff behind him acting as a sounding-board. A ten-mile range is common, and they can do fifteen if the atmosphere is favourable. There, he's finished," Frank added as the drummer struck a single sharp note and began to descend.

"They come," Kalubi reported as he rejoined them. He laid down the drum and went on: "Out on the flat below the mouth of the ravine stands a great baobab tree from which the lightning tore one arm. They will be there when the sun is high."

Frank remembered having noticed the damaged giant as he followed the koodoo into the cleft. "But why there?" he asked. "Aren't they coming up to get our loads?"

"It is the spot to which food and offerings are always brought. No man ever passes one step beyond it, lest the spirits slay him."

"Oh, curse those spirits," Frank ejaculated in English to Mansfield; "they might be a bit more reasonable! That'll mean we'll have to lug our stuff down there ourselves. Well, there's no help for it, so I suppose we'd better set about it."

He turned to say a few parting words to Kalubi, but the witch-doctor had already vanished inside his hut and had closed the wicker door firmly behind him.

CHAPTER EIGHT

MAC

WITH their backs against the vast bole of the damaged baobab, Frank and Mansfield sat amid their bundles of kit. Except for the faint rustling of the breeze in the surrounding tree-tops, and the persistent querulous calling of a pair of pied hornbills among the branches overhead, the bush lay silent and brooding under the mid-day sun. Frank thought regretfully of the coolness of the cave, and even of the chilly water of the pool, for not only had his clothes long since dried, but they were beginning to stick to him from the heat.

"When are these beggars going to turn up?" Mansfield growled for the third time.

Frank's only reply was a yawn; he knew the answer as little as his companion.

At last both men raised their heads. The sound of voices and footsteps had reached their ears, and presently a file of natives came in sight between the trunks.

The leader approached and saluted. "I am Mawanza," he announced. "The Keeper of the Spirits ordered us to come, and we are here."

Frank liked the look of him at once. For one thing, he was taller than the average, and his deep chest and thick arms spoke of considerable strength, while the dark eyes that, from beneath jutting brows, looked Frank straight in the face spoke of determination and character. His sole garment was a couple of yards of trade calico twisted lightly round his waist, and in his hand he carried a thin-bladed spear and a light axe.

Frank returned the salute and spoke of what he required of them, adding what the wages would be.

Mawanza dismissed the matter of wages with a gesture. "If the masters wish to make us a gift at the end of the journey, we will take it," he said in his deep voice. Clearly the subject did not interest him. He and his companions had come in obedience to the call they had received, and their reward would be Kalubi's approval and the protective influence of the unseen.

While the men adjusted their loads Mansfield asked Frank what he thought of the new carriers.

"A good lot, especially Mawanza," Frank replied. "He may not be exactly a beauty—indeed, that heavy jaw and those deeply ridged eyebrows give almost a touch of gorilla to the face—but he'll prove a very different lad from Taka. I can't see this chap chucking his hand in over some trivial thing."

Towards evening, according to Frank's estimate, the travellers passed out of British territory and made their first camp in Portuguese East Africa. The moment when they crossed the actual frontier was unknown to them, for the concrete obelisks that mark it, erected by the boundary survey expedition many years ago, stand four or five miles apart amid the encircling bush, and they did not happen to strike directly upon one of them.

The country on the Portuguese side was of much the same type as that which they had been traversing: closely growing forest covered the gently undulating ground, while here and there the sandy bed of a dry water-course, fringed by bigger timber along its banks, intersected their trail.

It was on the morning of the second day after leaving

the hills that an encounter occurred that was to have a far-reaching result on the fortunes of Frank and Mansfield.

The party were trudging along the sandy bed of a dried-up river—a way that offered the most direct route through a belt of bush pierced only by a maze of elephant and rhino paths. They were moving in almost complete silence, their footsteps deadened by the soft sand. Frank and Mansfield, at the head of the string, rounded a curve of the river-bed, and on the sloping bank saw three or four camp-fires whose blue smoke rose vertically into the still air. Around them several natives were squatting on their haunches, some cooking and others cutting up meat and cleaning a pair of fresh elephant-tusks, while beneath a shady tree lay a white man smoking a pipe.

One of the natives turned his head and caught sight of the approaching party. He promptly gave the alarm, and instantly there was pandemonium. The natives seized their spears and axes; the white man sprang from his blankets, snatched up a double-barrelled rifle, and brought the weapon to his shoulder.

Frank promptly threw up both hands and called out. He spoke no Portuguese, and for all he knew the man was one of that nation, but his exclamation in English seemed to have its effect. A look of relief appeared on the man's features, and slowly he lowered the muzzles of his heavy-bore weapon and made a sign to his followers.

"Ye're British, are ye?" he shouted. "Ah weel, then ye're no' what I thought. Come along up and let's hae a look at ye."

Frank and Mansfield ascended the bank. After a moment's further scrutiny the man laid down his rifle and held out his hand.

"My name's Macdonald," he said, "though most call

me just Mac. Sit ye down on that," he added, indicating his own primitive bed; "ye'll be thirsty, and they'll be brewing up some tea whiles. Losh, but ye nearly got a couple o' bullets in ye, coming up silently like that!"

Frank and Mansfield did as they were bidden, wondering why their soundless approach along the sand had caused such consternation to their host. Meanwhile the carriers laid down their loads and mingled with the other natives round the fires.

Macdonald must have known what was passing in the minds of his guests, for he went on: "Y'see, I thought ye were a party o' them Porti-goose police."

"Well, we're not," Frank laughed. "In fact we haven't seen anyone except natives for weeks."

"Oh aye, maybe there's none of them about, but I canna be too careful." He grinned, showing some damaged teeth, and poked Frank in the ribs with his fore-finger. "It's a verra sad thing, but in the eyes of the law I'm a criminal, though I'll no' say it worries ma conscience any." He glanced meaningly at the pair of fresh tusks that his natives had been cleaning, and winked.

Frank began to see light. Mac was clearly engaged in the risky but profitable pastime of elephant poaching, infringing several solemn edicts, both national and international, in the process, and laying himself open to a heavy fine and almost certain imprisonment.

Presently they made as if to continue their journey, but Mac would not hear of it. "Ye'll bide the night at least," he said. "I've no' spoken ma own tongue for weeks. What's the hurry? Whatever your business may be in these parts, to-morrow's as guid as to-day in this country, and better, as ye'll find out when ye've been as long in it as I have."

After a glance at Mansfield, Frank agreed. It occurred

to him that a brief delay might be profitable, for this man might know something of Oglethorpe. He sought an opportunity to tell Mac about their quest, but the poacher, after so long with only the companionship of natives, was too full of chat to give an opening. Frank knew that it would come in time, however, and meanwhile it would not be politic to force his way in.

"I'm from Scotland maself," Mac was saying; "maybe ye've no' been there, being southerners, I take it. Near Kingussie it was that I was brought up as a bairn."

Mansfield here remarked that he had once been there.

Mac's face brightened. "Have ye so? A gr-rand country, and the best deer forests in Scotland nearby. My dad was a ghillie on one o' them, and I was brought up to his calling. But the auld laird died, and a city man frae Manchester bought the place."

He shook his head sadly.

"I had yin look at him, and that was enough. I telled him I'd no' stop even if he offered me double wages, which he did. So I pulled out, and I've no' regretted it."

Frank smiled. "There's an old saying that a one-time poacher makes the best gamekeeper, and you've reversed the proverb."

"Aye that's yin way o' putting it. Each is a fine training for the other. It makes a man notice little things, and it's the little things that count."

"A risky profession, though," Frank commented, "spending your life dodging the police all the time."

"Not all the time. Poaching elephants is just a divairsion, a wee lapse from virtue that every man must have whiles. 'Minds me of ma dad's brother, a minister o' the kirk, no less, and verra strict. Once a year he would go away on a holiday, and it chanced that we heard he had been seen one night in the stalls of a Glasgow theatre.

After his preaching against all kinds o' worldly pleasure we couldna understand it, and when he came back ma dad tackled him.

"'Ah, Tammas,' says the minister reprovingly, 'how can I rail against the evils o' wasting good siller on idle amusements if I dinnae ken what they look like? I feel stronger and better for the contrast. Physic may be ill-tasting, but it does a body guid,' says he, looking solemn, but I could see a' the time there was a wee twinkle in his eye."

"So that's the side of the family you take after?" said Mansfield with a laugh.

"Ay. I'm verra respectable nine months o' the year. I travel round the villages, selling things to the black heathen, ye ken. Bringing light into dark places in the shape o' packets o' needles, and matches, and stretches o' calico to wrap round themselves. 'Tis no' an intellectual occupation, maybe, that of a travelling hawker; but there's nigh as much profit in it as there is in poached ivory. What's more the one helps the other."

"How's that?" Frank asked.

Mac winked. "What ivory hae ye seen in this camp? One pair o' tusks, and if ye'd come an hour later ye wouldna even hae seen those. Up north we're born careful, ye ken. I bury each pair as soon as they're cleaned. Later, when I'm moving from village to village, bringing the blessings o' ceevilisation to the savage, I collects 'em on the quiet, see? What Porti-goose policeman would think o' searching for ivory amongst the loads of grain and produce that a poor hard-working hawker, who takes out his licence regular, has traded in exchange for goods? It's tons I've passed under their noses in ma time."

Mac paused, giving Frank his opportunity. He realised that a man such as this must know the district thoroughly, and would be a most likely source of information about Oglethorpe. Leading on from the subject of Mac's wanderings, Frank gave a brief account of the reason that had brought himself and Mansfield to the spot.

Mac shook his head. "I canna mind such a body. Two year or more ago, ye say? Maybe he's here in these parts, but I've no' heard o' him. Had he any money? Always carried a full wallet, ye say? Then maybe he's no' lingered hereabouts, but pushed on." With a Scot's accuracy for the points of the compass, Mac jerked a thumb eastwards, towards the down-river settlements and the distant coast. "Unless he's never got through, and died in the bush," he added as an afterthought.

"Either might be possible, but we want to find out," said Frank.

"I'll tell ye what ye'd best do," Mac went on. "We're no' so far from the Zambezi itself; it's only a matter o' half a day's march awa' to the north o' us here. On the other side, maybe four or five mile back from the river, there's a man who runs a trading store. Pieters is his name—a body from the Cape. South African, ye understand. He's more likely to ken than anyone; he gets a' the news o' the district through passing customers bringing grain to trade."

"That's an idea," Mansfield put in.

"Ay, ye canna do better—if he's still alive, that is, for last time I had a crack wi' him, maybe three years back, he was as full o' fever as a native's dog is of fleas."

Mac turned his head and called a question to one of his natives.

"Aye," Mac went on when he had received his answer, "yon hunting-boy o' mine says the store's still running, so I reckon Pieters ain't dead yet. He says he heard from a passing savage who was buying there last week. So if ye'll tak' my advice ye'll go an' see Pieters. But ye must no' blame me if your welcome's no' to your liking."

"Why so?"

"He's a cross-grained sort o' de'il, as might be expected, not having been brought up in a ceevilised country," Mac went on, with the proud insularity of the Scot. "He's about as friendly to strangers as a crofter's dog chained up all day in a kailyard; but if ye say I told ye to come, like enough ye'll be for finding out what ye want."

The suggestion seemed too good to be ignored, and as Frank and Mansfield had already promised Mac they would keep him company that night, they planned to start direct for the Zambezi and the trader's store beyond it at sunrise the following morning. But, as it happened, their plans had to be altered somewhat.

That evening Frank noticed that Mansfield was looking far from well. He ate hardly anything, and, though the air was warm, he had fetched a blanket from his pack to wrap round his shoulders. When questioned he admitted that he was feeling rotten. Frank, knowing that Mac had a far greater experience of the country than he had, asked the older man to have a look at his companion.

"How long hae ye been in Africa?" Mac asked as he bent over Mansfield's crouching and shivering form. "Only a month or twa, eh? Then it's no' a touch o' malaria ye've got, for it takes longer than that for these an-anopheles germs"—he rolled the word lovingly on his tongue—"to work in your blood. Ye've taken a wee bit chill. Ye'll no' be travelling to-morrow or the next day, I'm thinking; for ye'd best lie up if ye dinna want complications."

Frank felt that he was right, though Mansfield protested that he would be well enough in the morning.

"Ye will not!" Mac retorted. And then he voiced something that was already in Frank's mind. "For why must the two o' ye go to Pieters' store? Stop along o' me and I'll look after ye, while your friend here goes north."

"It's a jolly good idea, and I've been thinking the same," said Frank. "The rest will do you good, Mansfield. I'll leave you here with most of the stores and carriers, and just take something for myself, and Mawanza to carry it. It's not far, and I'll be back in a couple of days."

As Mansfield still protested, Mac broke in: "Aye, o' course ye're stopping along o' me. Trouble? Huh! Dinna haver, laddie. It'll be no trouble at a', and if it was, d'ye think I'd mind? You do what I tell ye."

Mansfield began to thank their poacher friend, but Mac cut him short.

"Get doon between your blankets and I'll bring ye a drink whiles, with something in it. 'Tis nought but Porti-goose brandy, and poor stuff at that; 'tis no' like the Highland Dew that Andra Fraser keppit in the auld days, but it'll warm ye up and make ye sleep."

With a grunt the kindly Scot turned away to rummage among his stores.

CHAPTER NINE

IN the pearly light of the dawn Frank left the poacher's camp. He carried his rifle hitched over his shoulder by the sling, while behind him tramped Mawanza's stalwart form, Frank's roll of blankets and supplies perched on his woolly head and his spear in his hand. As he walked Mawanza crooned a little song of his own devising. His cheerfulness reflected itself in Frank, who felt that Mansfield's illness, though unpleasant for the sufferer, was probably for the best. He knew that alone he could travel more quickly than with the whole party, and meanwhile he was leaving his employer in good hands.

There were many signs of elephants in the bush through which they moved—Mac had certainly chosen a good spot for his law-breaking. Trees, smashed by the great beasts as they fed, lay across the narrow track, and spoor everywhere marked the sandy soil. Twice they heard the animals—the sharp crack of breaking branches and the shrill protest of some calf being reproved by its mother; but the bush was too thick to catch sight of the herds themselves. Nor did Frank specially want to. They might resent his presence in their domain, and Frank's job was to push on, and not go looking for trouble with some angry tusker.

As they pressed forward the ground began to take a definite downward trend, and Frank knew they could not be far from the river, though the surrounding trees made it impossible to see more than a few yards ahead. They covered another mile or two, and then the bush suddenly ceased, like the dividing of a curtain, and the view in front was revealed.

Frank found himself standing on the edge of a little brow of ground. Below him lay a sea of deep green reeds, whose myriad twelve-foot stems, crested with feathery plumes of pale cream, swayed slowly to and fro as the breeze passed over them in waves. In the middle distance stretched a broad band of brilliant blue—the Zambezi itself; and beyond rose, faint and indistinct in the heat haze, the hills of the northern shore.

The sea of reeds was clearly an impenetrable barrier. Frank glanced at Mawanza for his suggestions.

Mawanza pointed to the left. "We must go this way, master," he said in his deep voice. "We shall come to an open flat which stretches down to the water, and a village where they have canoes."

The two turned, keeping along the edge of the little brow that divided the higher bush from the lower reed-beds, and which, during the rainy months when the Zambezi spreads itself over miles of country, would form its seasonal bank. Presently, as Mawanza had said, the reeds tailed out into park-like flats, fringed by vegetable-ivory palms and dotted with huge m'sangu trees. A little way ahead, crowning a projecting cape of the higher ground, appeared the conical thatched roofs of a small village.

As they came nearer Frank noticed that the place looked deserted. He could see no smoke of cooking-fires or moving figures among the huts. He threw a question over his shoulder.

Mawanza confirmed his opinion. "These people are fishermen," he said. "They only live yonder when the country is under water. Now, when the river is low, we shall find them on its brink."

He was right. Striking across the open flats, they encountered a connecting path that led to a group of temporary shelters standing a few yards back from the water.

As Frank and his follower approached, women stopped their work and straightened themselves, pot-bellied children scattered in sudden shyness, and, despite the heat of the day, the headman dived into his hut to fetch a tattered military overcoat in which to receive his white visitor with becoming dignity.

The headman was most apologetic. Yes, there were canoes, plenty of them, but the young men were all away fishing. They would return sometime during the afternoon, and the first canoe to arrive should be at the white man's service. Meanwhile—

Frank nodded. He would just have to wait, and anyway it was close on noon, and he was hungry. He crossed over to the shade of a nearby tree and stood his rifle against the trunk, while Mawanza set about preparing food.

Seated under the leafy canopy, Frank looked out over the Zambezi. Though at that season of the year the river was almost at its lowest, at that point it was quite half a mile wide, a sparkling sheet that reflected the azure of the cloudless sky.

Here and there sandbanks, exposed by the falling level, appeared like yellow islands amid the blue, and on some of them Frank could see the long, dark shapes of crocodiles dozing on the sand while the hot sun warmed their backs. Those innocent of basking crocodiles were covered with birds. White egrets lined the crest of one like a snow-drift; another formed a resting-place for a flock of spur-winged geese. Spoonbills, herons, and a few glossy ibis moved sedately along the lip of the water; and high overhead a pair of fish-eagles circled endlessly, ready to drop like a stone on any luckless fish that should venture too near the surface of the river.

The circle of shadow beneath the tree became a lengthening oval, and still there was no sign of the canoes. At last Frank made out a distant dot, followed by a couple more, that rapidly grew larger as the paddlers made for home. One after another they bumped against the sandy bank, whereupon the women of the village hastened down with baskets to remove the fish that had been caught.

Zambezi canoes are dug-outs, each laboriously hollowed from a single trunk with primitive native adzes. The big m'sangu trees that grow so plentifully provide the material. Though somewhat clumsy in general appearance, these canoes are wonderfully steady afloat, owing to the shaping of the flat bottom, with a bilge-keel of heavy wood left at either side. Indeed, unless very carelessly handled, an upset is a rarity—an important point in a river that swarms with crocodiles.

The fish having been flung ashore and, under the head man's agitated directions, one of the canoes superficially cleaned out, Frank stepped aboard, followed by Mawanza and a couple of the fishermen. A dozen black hands pushed the vessel out from the shore, and the crew struck their long, leaf-shaped paddles into the water.

Squatting on the bottom—for a dug-out has no thwarts—Frank watched the bank recede. From his low position, hardly above the water level, the opposite shore appeared to have leaped back to the very horizon. The ripples slapped against the wooden sides of the dug-out and the steady pull of the current gripped its bottom

Dwarfed by the great expanse of the river, it seemed to Frank that the canoe had become infinitesimally small and unsafe. Meanwhile the two paddlers drove their vessel forward with vigorous strokes, chatting to Mawanza, and at the same time keeping a sharp lookout for any signs of hippo. A disgruntled hippopotamus, with its huge bulk and vast jaws, can constitute a real danger if it dislikes the look of a passing canoe.

At length Frank realised that the opposite shore, once so remote, was now close at hand. With a bump and a scrape and a swirl of water the dug-out grounded. After giving a small present to the men, he and Mawanza disembarked. They threaded their way through some patches of tall reeds and reached the higher ground, where another small village stood out against the background of bush.

Frank glanced at the sinking sun. Owing to the delay in getting the canoe, it was too late to think of pushing on. Finding a suitable spot, they made camp for the night.

The Zambezi was five or six miles behind them, and crowning a small rise in front stood the ramshackle cluster of pole-and-thatch buildings they had come to find.

Frank approached the store. A little group of native customers lingering outside made way for him as he came up, and he entered its dim and windowless interior. Coming from the bright sunlight, at first he could see nothing; though the smell of a typical bush store—a mixture of stiffly-sized calico, rolls of tobacco, and un-washed savage—enveloped him like a cloud. Presently his eyes became more accustomed to the murk. He made out a rough counter crossing the building lengthwise, and behind it the figure of a bearded white man who was regarding him with a pair of intolerant blue eyes.

"Er—good morning, Mr. Pieters."

"Who the blazes are you?" came the ungracious reply.

Mac's warning had prepared Frank for something of the sort, though not altogether for the speaker's appearance. He had visualised a far less robust-looking man; for Mac had said that when he had last seen him three years previously Pieters had been full of malaria. By his appearance now there was no doubt that he must have effectually shaken it off.

Frank gave his name and, as the poacher had advised him to do, mentioned Mac by way of introduction.

"Who's he?" came the gruff reply. "Don't know him from Adam, and don't want to."

"Well, he knows you," Frank retorted, "though I understand he's not met you for nearly three years."

The other's eyes narrowed. "Knows me, does he? I'll take his word for it; I can't be expected to remember every down-and-out Scottie I come across. Anyway, as I said before, where the blazes have you sprung from, and what do you want?"

"I'm looking for a man of the name of Oglethorpe."

The man behind the counter glanced up sharply, giving Frank a quick impression that this name at least was not entirely unknown to him.

"Oh, you are, are you? And what do you want to find him for? I know your kind. You're a police spy, I suppose, following up some poor devil that's made his getaway into Portuguese territory. Who do you think I am—Judas? Even if I knew him, you wouldn't catch me giving you a hint. Not much!" He laughed harshly.

Frank hastened to correct the false impression, relating a brief account of the facts of the case.

"Ho! So you and this Mansfield you talk about are trotting round trying to find someone and tell him he's come into money and will he please come home like a good little boy! Expect me to believe a yarn like that? I wasn't born yesterday, nor the day before, either. Now you take yourself off," the trader went on truculently, sticking out his chin so that his beard projected, "before I get over this counter and throw you out on your ear!"

Frank, who had already realised that his mission was a failure and was turning to go, faced round at the last words. Though the other might be the heavier man, he was not going to leave the building after a threat like that. "You just try it on!" he said defiantly.

The storekeeper let out a violent oath and was over the counter in one bound. Frank tried to keep him off with a straight left, but it was like hitting a tree. The next moment the two were locked in a savage tussle.

To and fro they swayed, bumping first against the wall and then against the rickety counter. The third bump was caused by the doorpost. Their feet caught in the sill, and the two men, locked in each other's arms, pitched through the doorway into the open.

It was the aggressor who fell undermost, striking his head on a stone. Frank felt the grip about him suddenly relax, and he rolled clear and scrambled breathless to his feet. But the other lay still, a thin trickle of blood running from his scalp.

Mawanza was the first to speak. "That was well done," he said, looking at Frank admiringly. "I have never seen white men fight before, though I have heard they can kill each other with their bare hands. Ah, see, he is stirring—strike him again before he recovers!"

Mawanza had no scruples about hitting a man when he's down.

Ignoring his unsporting follower, Frank held out a hand to help, but his late opponent thrust it aside and got to his feet. "I said I'd put you outside and I have," the man growled.

"Sorry about your head," said Frank. "Would you like me to bandage it before I go?"

"No."

"Very well then, I'll be off." Frank picked up the rifle he had leaned against the store wall, and turned.

"Wait a minute. Was that yarn you told me true?"

"Yes, it was, though I don't ask you to believe it."

"And you really want to find that fellow Ogle—Ogle-something?"

"Yes, and we mean to do so. If one line of inquiry doesn't work, we shall try another."

"Ah, well, I've been thinking it over again, and I'll give you a tip. You say you're not police, so I shan't be letting anybody down," he added with a leer.

Frank liked the look of him in this mood even less than he had in the former truculent one. However, Frank had come to get information, and he had been certain from the first moment that he had mentioned Ogle-thorpe's name that the storekeeper knew a good deal about him. This change of front might be a kind of belated apology for his former attitude. With a mental shrug Frank accepted it as such. "Well, what is it?" he said.

"It's only a tip, mind you, but you'd be wise to have a look round Makabi's village. From all I hear there's a white man living there on the quiet. You trot off and pay a call. From what you tell me, the sight of you and that pal of yours'll be as good as a drink to him," the trader added with another leer.

"Where is this place—near here?" Frank asked.

"About thirty miles away. See." With the stump of a pencil that he drew from the pocket of his shirt the storekeeper sketched a rough plan on the bare and dirty wood of the counter. "You go back and fetch that employer of yours, and start off *so*. Don't come here, whatever you do; it'll be miles out of your way. Cross the Zambezi again about *here*, and take this path, see? Any nigger'll tell you the way. And when you reach Makabi's I guess that'll be the end of your journey all right."

Frank gave a curt nod of thanks and left the store, Mawanza picking up his load and following in his tracks. As the two threaded their way back towards the river, Frank turned over in his mind what he had heard.

Though he disliked the informant, he felt that the information was probably correct. It fitted with what Mansfield had told him of Oglethorpe and his fear of being eventually traced and extradited to answer to the charge he still thought hanging over him. Frank could not help wondering, however, how Oglethorpe had managed to stand the life. From Mansfield's description the man did not appear to be of the kind that could stomach for long an existence where there would be little or no scope for his questionable talents. But fear is a great changer of character, and even in a remote native village he had probably found his opportunities.

It was late when they reached the Zambezi again, and they slept on the spot where they had spent the previous night, crossing over with the sunrise next morning to the southern bank.

Tramping at a good pace along the homeward track, Frank and Mawanza neared the elephant-poacher's camp. Frank wondered how Mansfield was; by now he should be almost recovered from his illness and fit enough to follow up the information gained.

Between the trunks Frank caught a glimpse of the greener foliage of the trees that lined the sandy river bed, and he gave a shout to herald his return. He did not hear any reply, but he remembered that probably both Mac and Mansfield would be dozing in the noontide heat, and the natives chattering and inattentive round their fires. A few more strides and he should see the smoke; but no blue wreaths became visible. Puzzled, Frank quickened his pace, and emerged from the trees on to the camping ground.

The white ashes of the cooking-fires lay cold and dead amid the flattened grass that the natives had used to sleep upon, and under the spreading tree, that had formed Mac's leafy home lay nothing but some broken boxes that had once contained stores. The place was silent and desolate. Its former occupants, both white and black, had vanished completely.

CHAPTER TEN

FOR a moment or two Frank stood motionless, staring at the dead ashes and the scattered debris of the camp. What on earth had happened? Even if Mac had suddenly wanted to move to a better locality for elephants, he would hardly have done so after volunteering to look after the sick man. And what had happened to Mansfield himself and their own natives? Even with Mac gone, Mansfield would have remained on the spot awaiting Frank's return.

Something unexpected had made them shift, but what? Ah, a sudden thought struck him, and Frank crossed over to the tree under which their blankets and stores had lain, fully expecting to find an explanatory note pinned to the trunk. But no scrap of folded paper greeted his eye, nor did one lie at its foot, dislodged by the breeze. Only the broken boxes dotted the ground—and why broken? One box, empty, might have been abandoned, but the others would have been needed to carry their contents.

Meanwhile Mawanza had put down his load and was taking a meditative pinch of snuff. Having sniffed it up to his satisfaction and sneezed a couple of times, he began to quarter the camp site, stooping here and there to touch the white ashes or to study the dry earth and sand for tell-tale spoor.

"Well, Mawanza, what do you make of it all?" asked Frank at length.

"They have gone many hours," the stalwart carrier replied, "for the ashes of the fires are quite cold."

"Yes, but why did they go?"

"Because they had to," Mawanza replied.

"Had to?" Frank repeated. "Why should they have to? What should make them leave so unexpectedly?"

Mawanza pointed to the earth. "Look, master, here, and again here. The marks of boots, not of the kind that the hunter of elephants wore, nor of those of the other with hair the colour of a bushbuck's coat. See, they were shod heavily with iron."

Mawanza widened the circle of his search, examining the fringes of the surrounding bush and dropping also on to the sandy bed of the river. Presently he returned.

"There were three white men in boots," he reported, "and six or seven black people with them. They came silently along the soft sand." He mimicked a crouching stalker. "It must have been after dark had fallen and when the camp lay asleep, for where they dislodged some stones under the shadow of the bank where the sun has not yet reached, the ground beneath them is still damp with evening dew."

Frank's thoughts immediately jumped to the time of his first arrival at that spot, and of Mac's alarm and subsequent explanation. Had the Portuguese police suddenly descended on the camp? It looked like it. But, even so, where was Mansfield? They might have arrested Mac and taken him away, but Mansfield had nothing to do with the illegal shooting of elephants. Yet there was no sign of him either, nor had he even left a note to say where he had gone.

As Frank puzzled over the matter he heard Mawazna give a gruff exclamation. From the cover of the bush a black face was peering in their direction.

Mawanza gave a reassuring shout. A look of relief crossed the man's features and he stood up. Frank recognised him as one of Mawanza's former companions, and as he approached, the rest of the party emerged from their sundry hiding-places.

"Now we'll get to the bottom of things," murmured Frank and began to question the foremost native.

"Yes, master, it was the police—three Portuguese and a number of down-river natives in uniform and armed with guns. They would never have found the place by day, but in the darkness the gleam of a camp-fire can be seen from far, and the hunter of elephants had ordered that big ones should be made to keep away the prowling beasts of the night."

Frank nodded. So he had been right in his surmise, and Mawanza's diagnosis of the numbers and time had also been correct.

"We were all asleep when they came, moving without sound over the soft sand, and the camp was filled with them before we woke. They seized the hunter of elephants before he could lift his big gun, and though he struggled and shouted many fierce-sounding words at them, they held him at last and locked iron rings on his wrists. The other, the red-headed one, they took more easily, for he was sleeping heavily, that one."

"But he had nothing do with the matter they had come about," Frank commented.

"I think he tried to tell them so, but they did not understand his words."

That would be so, Frank reflected, for, like himself, Mansfield knew no Portuguese. "And you?" he went on aloud.

"The master may remember that we slept on the far side of the camp, beyond the others and close to the bush.

We fled, diving amongst the trees, and though the down-river men ran after us, we were not caught. We hid till the coming of the dawn, and then crept back, to find only silence and emptiness, for the police had gone and taken everything. We hid again, and presently heard voices, but it was not until Mawanza shouted that we knew it was our own master returned."

Frank turned to Mawanza, who had already shown himself an accurate reader of signs. "Which way did they go after leaving here?" he asked.

"So!" Mawanza pointed without hesitation or any need to look for spoor. "When a man nets a buck does he not carry it straight to his village? They have made straight for their townships where they keep their prisons, where they hang those they catch, after the white man's fashion," he added complacently. "But we can make sure. There is a small village not an hour from here, and the people there will have seen them pass."

They had, as Frank and his followers discovered when they reached the place and questioned the head man. The party, he said, had passed through a little after sun-rise, with two dishevelled white men and several native trackers and carriers as prisoners. They were making for a point on the bank of the Zambezi, lower down-stream, where he had been told that a white man's chuff-chuff-canoe was moored, and by now they would be on the water, moving faster than any fish could swim.

So that was that, thought Frank to himself. He now had the whole sequence of events, and it remained only for him to decide on his own course of action.

Naturally there was but one open to him. Though he might not be able to do anything in Mac's case, he must follow up and endeavour to help Mansfield from the predicament in which his presence in the poacher's camp had involved him.

The police and their captives had gone down-river in, presumably, the launch which had brought them up to these parts. What was their destination? Probably Tete, the capital of the province, and that was quite a hundred and fifty miles away, possibly more.

Frank looked ruefully at the little package that Mawanza had been carrying on his head—all that remained to him, now that the stores of the expedition had been captured and taken away. Still, he could manage. He had his rifle and a handful of cartridges with which he could shoot meat, and eventually he would reach a place where flour and tea and sugar could be obtained. The main problem was the route.

The police had gone by water, but they had a fast launch. Frank might follow, reach the river bank, and get a canoe, but he felt certain that this would be unlikely for such a journey. He would have to have paddlers who knew the Zambezi, and these, not without reason, would shy at the idea of visiting a far township where they might be commandeered for Government work and be unable to return to their homes for many months. There remained walking. Frank shrugged his shoulders. He had done plenty already, and a few score miles extra would not hurt him.

Frank inquired of the head man about the country in front, and got nothing of value, for few of the villagers had ever travelled more than ten miles from their huts. Nor was Mawanza at all helpful; he, too, knew only his own district, and Frank realised that he would just have to push ahead and trust to luck.

Having arranged that the other carriers should remain at the village until he could get in touch with them again,

Frank struck out eastwards. He took Mawanza with him, more for companionship than anything else, for there was very little to carry.

Two days later they struck a road. It was the most primitive kind of track imaginable, full of projecting tree-stumps that nobody had bothered to root out; but it actually bore the marks of wheels, and where wheels had passed, wheels might come again. There was nothing to tell where the road came from or whither it went, but Frank followed along it and hoped for the best.

His luck was in. The two had not gone more than a few miles when they heard a sound behind them. They halted and turned.

The noise increased, and presently a lorry came in sight, bumping its way forward over the stumps. Seeing a white man waiting in the middle of the track, the driver pulled up, thrust a sallow and unshaven face out of the cab, and said something in Portuguese.

Frank made a gesture to imply that he did not understand, and answered in English, helping out his speech by signs.

The driver's lips parted in a cheerful grin. "Ah, you Breetish, eh? I gif you pick-up, eh?"

He opened the door of the cab invitingly, and Frank climbed aboard, while Mawanza scrambled up on to the pile of sacks that filled the back of the truck. The driver noisily re-engaged his gears, and the lorry bumped ahead once more.

Frank settled himself on the hard seat, his rifle against his knees, and in the quieter moments between the crashes and squeaks of the springs remarked that he was lucky to have struck someone who could understand English.

"Ah, yas, I spik him well as Breetish man," the driver replied complacently. "I travel many country and I learn. I not like these Portuguese who stay one place; I Grik, yas."

Frank had already suspected as much, for there are many Greeks in Africa; indeed, it might be said that the British and the Greeks are the only two peoples that leave the settled areas behind them from choice.

"How far you go?" the driver went on.

"I'm trying to get through to Tete."

"Tete? That is much far!" The Greek took both hands from the steering-wheel and waved them dramatically to stress the point; and the lorry immediately seized the opportunity to swerve violently towards the nearest tree-trunk. "But you have much luck," he went on, "for I, I go also to Tete, and I the best driver in the country, yas."

Frank wondered grimly what the others could possibly be like.

"I come from *prazo*—what you call farm, eh?—over there." Once more his hands left the wheel while he indictated the road behind. "I take in sack that they sell to merchant in Tete. You know town, no? Fine place, but I like him not—too much official, too much police, yas."

At the mention of police Frank felt that he had better tell his companion something of his own circumstances, for no doubt the man could give him some useful tips.

"Not good lucks for your friend," was the driver's opinion. "The elephant-shooter, if they have catch him red-hand, will make long time in prison or big fine. And the other, you say he nothing to do with it; but if can, they find something against him. Have he done anything wrong? Have he entered country without visa to passport, or brought in firearms without permit, no?"

Frank started. It was exactly what he and Mansfield

had done! When they set out originally he had not anticipated that their wanderings would lead them outside British territory, and until now he had entirely forgotten those international regulations.

The Greek read the look on Frank's face.

"He have, eh? Then he get trouble too." The speaker eyed for a moment the rifle that Frank held between his knees, and added, "You got permit to have him?"

"No, I haven't, I'm afraid. To tell the truth, I never thought about it until just now."

"And you carry him for all mans to see! We must change him quick, before we go one kilometre farther, yas."

The Greek brought the lorry to a standstill, jumped down, and began to fumble in his tool-box. He produced a screw-driver. "Give him me," he said, holding out his hand for Frank's weapon.

The man might not be a good driver, but he was neat with his hands. With a few deft movements he detached the barrel from the stock, halving the rifle's length. He reached for Frank's bundle of blankets that Mawanza had dumped beside him on the load, and undid the straps. Carefully he placed the barrel and stock inside as a kind of core, and restrapped the blankets in a neat roll.

"That better," he commented as he tossed them aboard again. "Now you not carry firearm. Roll of blanket not interest them, no. Police think not long enough, end would stick out. You safe as bank now, yas."

As the lorry progressed the road got better, for it was joined by other branches, and its greater use had necessitated the removal of the worst of the stumps. Meanwhile Frank's companion chatted on, giving him some sound advice.

"When arrive, you go straight to good 'otel. No

money? What matter, 'long as they not ask pay in advance. Police not interested in stranger at good 'otel; too many passing through."

Frank realised the wisdom of the suggestion. Tete was the point where the motor road from Rhodesia to Nyasaland crossed the Zambezi by ferry, and with many strange faces in the lounge and bar and street outside, there was little likelihood of any awkward questions. Motorists would have passed that ordeal already at the roadside posts on the southern or northern frontiers.

"From 'otel call quick on Breetish Consul," the driver went on. "His job to see police, that what he paid for. He good man. Sometime he act for us when Grik consul away. Once I met him, yas, when chief of policeman arrest me for running into wall; he make them see it fault of fool woman in middle of road who can't make up mind which way to run."

The reminiscences rambled on, while steadily the road became better. Crops and farmhouses were passed, and at last they came in sight of Tete, its white buildings dotting the level ground between the wide Zambezi in front and the massive bulk of Carrueira Mountain behind.

The lorry rumbled into the town—one of the oldest European settlements in Africa, for it was founded by the Portuguese adventurers who ascended the Zambezi with sword and arquebus, helmet and plate armour, about the year 1540, and Portugal has maintained a small garrison there since 1632. Frank's Greek friend dropped him and Mawanza—who was staring with awe at the white man's strange buildings—in front of the hotel, and drove off, waving both hands out of the window, the lorry careering from side to side amid the curses of those who sprang hastily out of the way.

While Mawanza waited outside, scared of his surroundings for the first time in his life, Frank boldly entered the hotel and demanded a room. He knew that he presented a very different aspect from the neat motorists who usually frequented the place, but he hoped that the clerk would take him for some eccentric traveller who did not care about his appearance in a foreign country. His bluff succeeded. Without any question of payment in advance Frank got his room, while a native servant was sent to retrieve Mawanza from the street and take him round to the appropriate quarters provided at the back.

Frank's first thought was to have a bath and make himself reasonably presentable. Feeling much better after a thorough clean up, he put a good meal inside him, and then went to the office to inquire the way to the British consulate. He received his directions, and stepped out again into the wide street.

CHAPTER ELEVEN

ESCUDOS ARE NOT POUNDS

WHEN Frank reached the consulate he received his first setback. He found that the Consul was away on a short but well-earned holiday, and would not be back for about three weeks. Would Frank call round again then?

No, he wouldn't! Frank knew there must be someone acting in the Consul's absence, and his persistence at length unearthed him.

The man behind the desk was annoyed. He was only there temporarily, and he had hoped to shelve anything unpleasant during his brief term of office. He looked disapprovingly at Frank through a pair of thick-lensed spectacles, yawned, and asked him what he wanted. Frank never learned his name, but he mentally christened him "Percy the Pip-squeak."

Frank had not been offered a seat, but he took one, for his tale would occupy some time, and he did not intend to be summarily dismissed. At length he completed his statement.

"You say," commented 'Percy' with another yawn, "that your friends are now in the custody of the Portu-guese police, and presumably lodged in the jail here. I have heard nothing of such an arrest and detention."

Frank felt like replying, "Then you should have done —it's your job to know these things," but he decided to refrain for the present.

"You say this man Macdonald is charged with poaching elephants," Percy went on. "Now, that is a serious matter and one in which I cannot interfere. The laws of this country must take their course. In the matter of your employer, Mansfield, however, there may be extenuating circumstances, and no doubt, if what you tell me is correct, he may be able to prove himself innocent of aiding and abetting."

"If he could prove himself innocent he wouldn't need your intervention on his behalf," Frank put in sourly.

Percy looked pained, wishing once more that the Consul was not absent. No doubt he knew how to deal with this kind of person who failed to show respect to an official, however acting and temporary.

"You see," Frank explained, "though he has nothing to do with the poaching they'll probably bump him for possessing a rifle without having obtained an import licence. The fact is that we forgot all about such things when we crossed the border."

Percy looked horrified at such a lapse of memory. "That also is a serious matter," he said, "but no doubt a fine will meet the case. I will get in touch with the authorities in the course of the next few days, and make inquiries."

But Frank was not taking his dismissal in that fashion. "During the next few days?" he snorted. "And what about my friends meanwhile, whom you didn't even know were in prison till I told you? What's wrong with right now?"

The other sighed. Much as he wanted to get rid of Frank, he feared that there might be trouble if news of his dilatory attitude reached the ears of the Consul on his return, and this young ruffian looked quite capable of making things unpleasant. He agreed with the best grace he could, and fetched his sun-helmet.

The two entered the police office, and were presently

received by the commandant. In the bored voice of
one who is the victim of unkind fate, Percy announced the
reason for their visit.

"Yes," said the commandant, speaking in excellent
English, "there are two men of that description here who
have been brought in from the up-river country. My
police do not often make mistakes, but of course there
may be circumstances we do not know about." His
glance turned to Frank. "I shall be glad to hear what you
have to tell me."

Frank liked the look of the commandant, for he was a
very different kind of person from Percy. The Portuguese official was alive, and a man with a sense of fairness and of his own responsible position. Though Frank
realised he dared say little about Mac's case until he knew
exactly how much the police had found out about his
transgressions, he could at least be open and candid in
the matter of Mansfield.

The commandant listened, and made several notes on
a pad before him. "Yes, I see," he commented; "it ap-
pears that this man was a victim of unfortunate circumstances, and I think that the charge against him of being
an accomplice will be dropped. But he was in possession
of a firearm without a permit. Yes, I know you told me
how this came about, but it still remains an offence.
However, a small fine will settle that. And now, if you
will excuse me, I have much to do."

Percy rose with alacrity and made for the door, thankful
to be rid of the business, but Frank lingered for a moment
to ask if he might be allowed to see the prisoners.

The commandant shook his head. "I'm afraid that is
against the regulations, unless you are a legal man, which
you are not. Pity your Consul isn't here—not that fool,
but the real man," he added, glancing towards Percy's

retreating back. "But don't you worry; there will be no delay, for the case will come up to-morrow, and I will see that both your friends get a fair hearing."

The following day Frank attended the trial, and once more set eyes on his friends whom he had last seen in the lonely jungle camp by the dry river-bed. As the prisoners glanced round the court they spotted him, and Frank saw surprise leap into their eyes. He could see them wondering how he had managed to follow so quickly and accurately, and he anticipated a volley of questions when they were once more able to have a chat together. Meanwhile the business of the day was beginning.

The proceedings were different in many ways from those of an English court, but despite his ignorance of the language, they seemed to Frank to be conducted with fairness. Mansfield's case came up first, and after examination through an interpreter, Frank himself was called as a witness. Judgment was then given, and the amount of the fine imposed almost made Frank's hair stand on end until he realised that the figures, in escudos, represented only about three-pounds-ten in British sterling.

Mac's case took longer, for there was more evidence against him. He fought warily, giving away no points to the enemy under questioning. He could not deny the one pair of tusks that had been found in his camp; but the prosecution could not fasten on him any proof of having shot more than that solitary specimen.

Mac played skilfully on the temptations that beset a wandering hawker who has to carry a weapon for safety's sake when wandering from village to village in elephant-haunted country, though he lost ground over the undeniable fact that no trading goods had been found among hit loads. Frank remembered, with an inward grin, what Mac had told him about the ivory he had hidden until it could be recovered quietly in the course of legitimate business, and he saw that Mac's Scottish caution was bringing its reward.

Even so, Frank expected that the sentence would be one of imprisonment, but Mac was given the option of a fine, and promptly accepted it. Mansfield's fine had seemed huge enough, but Mac's sounded perfectly appalling; however, a quick calculation from escudos to sterling told Frank that it was fairly moderate for the offence. Mac would still be left with a handsome profit from the hidden ivory, and no doubt he would continue his periodical lapses as before, merely taking greater precautions not to be caught.

The court rose, and Frank waited outside for his friends, who presently appeared, after having made arrangements about the payment of their fines. Arm in arm they made for the hotel, and called for drinks to celebrate their reunion.

As they listened to each other's recent adventures and spoke of their own a native waiter brought in an official-looking envelope and handed it to Frank. He tore it open, glanced at its contents, and as the humour of it struck him, began to laugh.

"Who's that from?" asked Mansfield.

"The commandant. It's really for you, as a matter of fact. As you have paid your fine, he's now sending you a permit to carry a weapon, and you can have your own rifle back if you'll call at the police station."

"So I should. I don't see there's anything funny in that."

"No, but this is." Frank held out a second paper. "A permit for me, too. He's a sportsman, that chap; he must have guessed I'd be likely to have a rifle hidden away somewhere, as I have, and he's sent this along as a kind of humorous dig in the ribs!"

"Aye, he's a good lad, yon commandant," Mac commented. "If there were more like him, this 'ud be a better country. And now," he went on, "ye've no' said how ye got on after ye left us. Did ye find the store?"

Frank grinned. "I found it all right, and its keeper too. You warned me to expect a cranky sort of fellow, and you were right."

"So Pieters is still alive?"

"I should say very much so—*and* kicking! We started with words and followed up with blows, but all the same I got something out of him in the end." Frank went on to relate the information he had gathered.

"That looks good enough," said Mansfield, "and the sooner we get to this place—Makabi's, did you call it?—the better."

Frank nodded. "We've got to replenish our stores first," he said, "and arrange for getting them up-country, for I left our carriers to await our return, and have got only Mawanza with me. I'll be needing some cash out of you, Mansfield; in fact I'm living here on tick at the moment."

"That's all right; I've a letter of credit that the local bank here will honour. But," he added as an afterthought, "what about those stores we had? The police ought to disgorge them."

"Ye've no' got a hope," Mac grinned.

"But it's scandalous," Mansfield broke out. "First I'm wrongfully arrested, and then my belongings are stolen—"

"Oh aye, maybe, but it's no' the British police ye're dealing with. Ye could ask the commandant, but I'd no' advise that; though he's a white man, he'd no go agin the custom o' the country. Ye'll be wise just to buy more."

"Oh, very well," Mansfield shrugged.

"And now I'll be after doing my own business," said Mac, rising. "I've no' got a letter o' credit or that sort o' luxury, and I've got to pay that fine inside three days. But I ken a crony o' mine here who'll lend me the doings until I return from my next journey selling things round the villages—and doing a wee bit o' digging whiles!" he ended with a wink.

After the recent misfortunes Frank felt that fate owed him a stroke of luck, and he was not disappointed. When out in the town he fell into conversation with the skipper of a tiny river steamer that was moored at the wharf, and he learned that she was due to leave on the morrow with goods for delivery at a Jesuit mission station upstream. Frank thought immediately of the chance of a lift, for her destination was more than half-way towards their own. He put forward the suggestion, and her master promptly agreed.

The following morning, therefore, Frank and Mansfield, together with Mawanza and the newly purchased necessities, went aboard, to find Captain Jones, in the usual river skipper's uniform of singlet and dungaree trousers, awaiting them. The accommodation was of the most limited description, but the vessel was clean and British owned, as the dingy Red Ensign hanging limply aft proclaimed. Like all vessels designed for shallow waters with many sandbanks, she was a stern-wheeler drawing only a few inches, and was flat-bottomed and broad in the beam. Indeed, she was not unlike a fat water-beetle with an upper deck fitted on its back and a long funnel projecting above all.

With stout poles her crew pushed her from the bank,

and in response to a tinny tinkle from her toy bridge, her Zanzibari engineer let steam into her wheezy and old-fashioned cylinders. The stern-wheel slap-slapped the water briskly, and she drew out into mid-stream.

No one would have called her fast, even in the days of her youth, and now, against the current of the river, she averaged hardly two knots. Every few hours she sidled into the bank alongside a pile of cut logs, and took aboard sufficient fuel to keep her going till the next wooding stage was reached.

Frank and Mansfield spent their time beneath the shadow of the upper deck, lazily watching the panorama of river scenery slide slowly past. During the daylight they saw little of the grey-headed skipper. Navigation claimed his whole attention, for the Zambezi continually changes its shallows and sandbanks, and where there was deep water one month there might be only a few inches the next.

Captain Jones was well aware of the dangers of running hard aground at that season of the year, with the water falling daily. Indeed, cases have occurred where a steamer has had to be abandoned till the coming of the rains. As it was, despite his watchfulness the vessel twice touched bottom, but with her stern-wheel thrashing in reverse, and the lusty shoves of her native crew, who had promptly jumped overboard, she was got safely off into deeper water.

At night, however, the passengers saw more of their skipper, for navigation was too risky after dark, and they spent from sunset to dawn tied up to the bank. They found him entertaining company, for he was full of yarns of the old days before roads and railways had killed water-borne traffic on the lower river between Tete and the distant coast.

Though the journey was a slow one, neither Frank nor Mansfield was sorry for the rest after the strenuous time they had been through, and before tackling the heavy days they saw in front of them. But these did not worry them overmuch; they felt that the end of their labours was in sight, forgetting the old proverb that Africa always has surprises in store.

At last the steamer reached her destination and tied up alongside a primitive wharf against the southern bank. Above it several white buildings with deep verandas crowned a rise of land, with a squat bell-tower leaning over them.

The Jesuits to whom the place belonged received Frank and Mansfield hospitably, detailing one of their number who spoke English to see to their wants. The stores were landed, together with the cargo which the vessel had brought, and a room in the tiny guesthouse was allotted to their use.

Their next step had already been fully discussed during their idle hours aboard the steamer. Frank despatched Mawanza to make contact with the carriers who had been left behind and bring them back with him. They would have to wait some days until the men arrived, but it would save time in the end, for the party could then strike out direct for the distant village where Oglethorpe was reported to be lurking in obscurity.

Frank and Mansfield found the English-speaking Jesuit, who was known as Father Manoel, an interesting companion, and during the talks they had with him they sought information about the route they should follow.

With the aid of a very inaccurate map in the possession of the community they were able to fix the approximate locality, for the position of Pieters's store appeared upon it, and the man with whom Frank had fought had said that Makabi's villages lay some thirty miles beyond it.

"It lies well back and north of river, eh?" Father Manoel commented. "You best cross Zambezi here— we have good boat—and travel so!" 'He traced a finger diagonally across the map towards the district Frank had indicated. "I know the country little way, yes, but not far; I will ask our natives if know beyond. But—" He paused.

"But what?" Frank asked.

"But I would not care go up there just now, unless under order from our Society, which different, of course."

"Why not?"

"Trouble brew up there. What trouble? How do I know? Grievance over tax, perhaps. We hear rumour that good modern firearm, not gaspipe of savage, appear among the people, and of a not-known white man some-where in area who supply them. Perhaps not true, but, as you English say, 'no smoke without a fire,' eh? Still, perhaps you safe, you not Portuguese or man belonging to Government. So far Government ignore rumour, but——" He shrugged his shoulders.

Mansfield immediately pricked up his ears.

"You don't say so! Then it's a fiver to a bent penny that my cousin—the fellow we're looking for—is up there, as we thought. Gun-running, the dirty dog, and making two hundred per cent. profit out of it, I'll bet. Just like him, that would be—pocketing the dollars and not caring two straws about those who'll have to face the music when a showdown comes."

"After what I heard at the store," Frank said, "I wondered how Oglethorpe could stick it in a remote village and not be bored to death. It looks now as if we know how he's been occupying himself."

"Sure thing," Mansfield agreed. "However, his games are nothing to do with us; that's for the local police to get hot and bothered about. What we're after is to make contact with him and get proof that he's still alive—or rather was at the time of my uncle's death. It's us for this Makabi place right away, and then back to civilisation and my lawyer's office at home."

CHAPTER TWELVE

THE STORM-CLOUDS GATHER

MAWANZA having returned bringing his five comrades, the party was again complete. Frank and Mansfield said good-bye to their hosts, and embarked in the broad-beamed iron boat that had been put at their disposal to take them across to the northern bank of the Zambezi.

Once more the trees of the forest swallowed them up, as in single file they tramped along the narrow track leading away from the river. Frank had no fears that they would lose their way during the first day or two, for Father Manoel had supplied very careful directions, but it was beyond that limit that they might have difficulty; however, they would be sure to strike villages where inquiries could be made. Frank had memorised the sketch made by the storekeeper on his dirty counter, but this was of little value, as they were aiming for Makabi's from an entirely different angle.

Away from the cooler breezes that played over the broad waters of the river the heat was intense, and even the hours of darkness brought little relief. When he had started originally Frank had not anticipated being away so long, and the rising temperatures warned him that the dry season was nearing its end, and that before very long the rains would be upon them.

Though it might be a little while yet, there were plenty of signs that could be read. The heat-haze had turned the sky as colourless as burnished steel and obscured any hill or other landmark more than a mile or so away. The bush lay lifeless, for at sunrise the wild creatures had all sought their shady lairs, and even the trees seemed to be wilting under the torrid rays. But life was there, awaiting the change of the season, for on every branch appeared the leaf-buds that would burst forth into luxuriant foliage as soon as the magic touch of the water moistened the parched soil beneath.

The moving column at length passed beyond the limit of Father Manoel's directions, and began to check their route by inquiries from any native they might meet. They got their information, but Frank could not help noticing that it was given grudgingly. It looked as if there was truth in the rumour they had been told, and that they were entering a disaffected area, especially as the surliness increased as they advanced.

Frank spoke of it to Mawanza, who made a gesture with his hand.

"Something bites them, like a flea under a man's loin-cloth, but I do not know what it is, master. These people beyond the great river are not of my tribe; indeed, in the old days before the coming of the white man our fathers fought with them often." He breathed a sigh in memory of a past that would never return. "If there were fifty of us with spears we could even now teach them a lesson they would not forget. As it is, they are like monkeys up a tree that chatter and grimace at a passing lion beneath, knowing they are safe. But the lion takes no heed, nor need we of these baboons without tails," he ended scornfully.

Though Mawanza might express contempt, the local attitude made Frank feel uncomfortable, for hitherto he had always found natives reasonably obliging, even when not actively welcoming. However, they were getting close to Makabi's group of villages, and he hoped that it would not be long before they were on their way back to a more friendly district.

Their destination proved to be a fair-sized village with several small offshoots, surrounded by a belt of cultivated land where the brown soil lay turned and ready for the planting season. Owing to the unfriendly attitude, already experienced, of the local people, Frank decided not to make camp close to the main village. After consultation with Mansfield, he chose a spot about half a mile from it, where a spreading tree stood in the middle of a small natural clearing. The tree would provide essential shade, and the open ground ensure that no stranger could walk in upon them unchallenged.

Mawanza nodded approval, muttering something about sneak-thief dogs instead of men, and added a suggestion that he and his fellow carriers should erect a boma, or circular fence of thorn bushes, around the camp. Frank had seldom done such a thing before, except in notorious lion country, but with a nod he agreed. They might be there some days, and he knew there are times when a stout fence can be a wonderful help towards a sound night's sleep.

Leaving Mawanza and his companions to chop down branches and erect the boma, Frank and Mansfield hooked their rifles over their shoulders by the slings and went off to interview the local headman.

They made their way across the cultivated land and reached Makabi's main village. The young men lounging among the huts, and the women engaged on their daily tasks, greeted them with insolent stares, and made no move to get out of the way. Frank and Mansfield, however, pointedly took no notice, and before their determined advance the natives sullenly moved aside.

Beneath a shady tree in the centre of the village squatted

a group of elders. Instead of rising to greet their visitors, as etiquette demanded, they remained aggressively seated, and one of them murmured something that raised a laugh.

Frank flushed angrily, but he was determined to keep his temper. "Which of you is the headman?" he demanded.

One of the group slowly turned his head. "He is away, far away, on a long journey."

Frank was certain that was a lie. He was no doubt actually one of the group, possibly even the speaker himself.

"I hear you say it," Frank retorted with a shrug. "The presence or absence of a petty chief matters nothing to us. You will do just as well. There is a white man living here or somewhere close by, and we want to speak to him."

"There is no white man here," came the sullen answer.

"We're not police, so you needn't think we've come here to make trouble," Frank went on patiently. "We have good news to give him."

"There is no white man here," the native repeated; "we do not want any such in our village." The speaker's tone clearly indicated that present company was not excepted.

Frank felt like hitting him, but he kept his hands to his sides. He tried again, taking a slightly different line, but was met by the same blank wall. He realised that he was getting no farther, and that persistence would probably do more harm than good. He made a sign to Mansfield, and the two turned away, ignoring the low sniggers of laughter that followed their retreat.

Mansfield made a forcible comment on the recent interview.

Frank nodded. "Yes, there's something pretty wrong with that lot; that rumour we heard about trouble brewing up was quite right. Also about them being supplied with modern firearms. I don't know whether you noticed, but I saw several good rifles resting against the walls of the huts we passed—things that don't grow on the nearest bush. There's someone behind all this, right enough."

"Yes, that cousin of mine, for a cert, and we're going to find him. I haven't come all this way to be put off by those black blighters. What's the next suggestion—search the neighbourhood ourselves?"

"We could, but it wouldn't be much use. We've got to think up something better. Meanwhile, let's get back to the camp."

On reaching it, Frank called for Mawanza and put the matter before him. "I want you to make friends with these people; keep your eyes and ears open, and find out what we want to know. You can give the impression that you're thoroughly discontented and want to desert, and that you'd like to join in with whatever they're planning. Don't overdo it, of course."

Mawanza's white teeth gleamed as he grinned broadly. "A man of my tribe to make friends with these baboons-without-tails! But as you ask it, master, I will do what I can. If we had fifty young men with us we would make them speak in a different fashion, for a red-hot spear-blade beneath the armpit will make the most stubborn talk! But as it is—" He made a gesture of resignation, and slouching his shoulders and putting on the expression of a potential deserter, he mooched off in the direction of the village.

Frank chuckled as he watched Mawanza's departure. "Natives are natural actors," he said to Mansfield, "and

Mawanza's no fool into the bargain. I'll back him to find out something of value before very long."

Mawanza was a quick worker, and in a day or two he was able to make his report.

"The white man you seek does not live here," he said. "He comes now and then, but I cannot learn where from. The guns are of his supplying, and though they complain of his high price, they take them, for they plan to use them on the Portuguese."

Frank nodded. "Yes, go on."

"There is much talk about your presence here, master, for they think that you are spies of the police, and the young men are clamouring that you shall be prevented from telling what you have seen. But the elders have restrained them so far, saying they must wait until they have had word from him who supplied the guns. Meanwhile they have sent a message to him."

"Ha!" Mansfield put in. "That may make him show up here, perhaps. We'll sit tight till he comes, that's what I say."

"As you wish but he may not come, after all; he may send a message instead," Frank replied with a shrug. He realised that the situation was beginning to look ominous, though clearly Mansfield had not grasped that fact. However, he did not wish to appear as an alarmist, and agreed to wait a little to see how things developed, wondering whether he was a fool not to insist on withdrawing from the area before any crisis arose.

The strain was physical as well as mental, for the trouble with the local natives was not the only crisis approaching. For several days the heat had been intense, the bush lying silent and desiccated under its impalpable canopy of haze; while by night the cloudless sky had been lit up every few seconds by the soundless flicker of sheet lightning. Apart from anything else, it was time to be gone, before the rains should turn the world into a quagmire and enormously increase the difficulties of reaching civilisation once more.

It was about an hour after Mawanza had made his report that the drums began.

Frank knew their significance, for it is a common custom in nearly every African village. They were "calling up the rain," and they would continue till the weather broke. But the people would not confine themselves to drumming; they would dance and drink quantities of sour native beer prepared specially for the occasion becoming excited almost to frenzy. In their present mood Frank realised the danger instantly, and decided that a move should be made first thing the following morning, however much Mansfield might object.

Night came on, and beneath the silent flickering gleams of the lightning the roar of the drumming increased. Frank slept fitfully, and he was not sorry to see the dawn begin to steal across the sky. As he lifted his head, he found Mawanza standing over him.

Mawanza was shaking with rage. "They've gone, all of them!" he exclaimed. "I thought they were my brothers, for they came from the same village, but now I see they are nothing but cowardly jackals and hyenas!"

Frank sat up, and as he looked round he understood what Mawanza was talking about. Except for Mansfield, still asleep, there was nobody else in the camp. Accurately reading the menacing voices of the drums and their probable sequel, the five other carriers had quietly crept from the boma during the night and fled to a safer locality.

Frank stirred up his sleeping companion, who was in no very good temper after what had been almost a quarrel the previous evening when Frank had delivered his ultimatum. But as he glanced round the deserted camp and took in what had happened, he began to realise that Frank had not been indulging in empty talk.

Meanwhile the man he had abused the evening before was pulling on his clothes and filling his pockets with cartridges.

"Come on, Mansfield, get busy. Strikes me the sooner we shift the better."

"But these?" Mansfield pointed in a slightly bewildered way to the loads of stores.

"We'll have to abandon them. No help for it. Just load ourselves and Mawanza with what food we can manage and hop it. We won't get those carriers back, and the longer we hang about here the more difficult it's going to become."

The words were hardly out of his mouth when Mawanza gave a grunt of surprise. Emerging from the bush was one of the absconding natives, bleeding from a spear-gash in the shoulder. He came up, shamefaced and panting, and Frank soon had his story out of him.

He and his companions, he admitted, had slipped away during the night, fearing what might happen. They had not gone more than a few hundred yards when they encountered a line of men waiting silently in the darkness. Though its occupants had not known it, the camp had been surrounded and picketed by the local natives.

They had tried to slip through the cordon in the darkness, the man went on, but they had been detected and chased. His four companions had been run down and speared, but he himself, though wounded, had managed to evade the pursuers, and finding himself headed back, had returned towards the camp.

"Do you mean to say those men have been killed?"

Mansfield stammered. His previous scepticism about what Frank had said was certainly coming home to roost.

"Yes, and some more are going to be before we're through with this business," Frank replied grimly, "and it's for us to see we're not next on the list."

"What do you suggest?" Mansfield had now pulled himself together after what had been a bit of a shock to his London-bred nerves. He was beginning to realise that there are still parts of the world where men can be speared light-heartedly.

"We must change our plan," said Frank decisively. "If those carriers, brought up in bush-craft, couldn't slip through in the darkness, we haven't a hope on earth of doing better in the daylight amongst all those close-growing trees. We should be ambushed immediately, and they have plenty of rifles, remember; I expect the reason they didn't use them just now was so as not to give the alarm to us. We'll have to stop here at least till to-night before making any attempt," he went on, though he knew success was more than doubtful.

"Meanwhile, do you think they'll attack us here?"

"I haven't an idea," Frank replied, "but anyway this spot gives us a chance. The thorn fence will stop a rush, and the open ground beyond will give us ample warning, and anyone trying to cross it'll get hurt." He turned to Mawanza. "Take an axe and get some more branches to strengthen the boma. Meanwhile you"—he signed to the wounded carrier—"let's see what I can do about your shoulder."

It was about an hour later when the steady roll of the drums, which had persisted since the previous afternoon, ceased with startling abruptness, and the bush lay silent under the heat, except for the endless humming of the cicadas and other insects amongst the undergrowth.

"Now what's the game?" Frank muttered, half to himself.

It was Mawanza who interpreted the sudden silence.

"The messenger that they sent to the white man who supplied them with their guns has returned," he said. "That dog of a headman and his elders will be even now deciding what they will do." He turned to pick up a flat stone, and with it began to hone the blade of his spear till its edges, already sharp, were like razors. "It will not be long now before we know," he added casually, as one who comments on the weather.

Frank and Mansfield followed his example, placing their stock of ammunition handy and testing the smooth action of their rifles. Meanwhile they listened intently, but not a sound other than those of nature came to their ears from beyond the encircling trees.

CHAPTER THIRTEEN

THE STORM BURSTS

THE silence remained ominous and brooding under the oppressive haze of heat.

Was an attack coming? Frank asked himself. Mawanza seemed certain that it would, but there might be quite a different development. What had been the message received by Makabi's people? Or had there been any message at all? It was only a guess to explain the abrupt cessation of the drumming. Perhaps the mysterious white man, whom he felt certain must be Oglethorpe, had arrived personally, in which case he might emerge at any moment from the trees, demanding to know what they wanted.

On the other hand, if Mawanza were right, any attack was likely to be in the nature of a surprise rush, with a view to catching the occupants of the boma unawares. It would probably come from the side nearest the villages; and sheltered behind the screen of branches, Frank and Mansfield kept watch in that direction, Mawanza and the wounded native keeping an eye on the other quarters.

The minutes dragged slowly, but still nothing happened.

Suddenly the silence was shattered by a ragged volley from the bush beyond the open ground, the bullets passing high over the heads of those within the boma. Few natives, unless trained, can shoot straight, even with modern rifles; they like to see the muzzles of their weapons well above their backsights when they pull the

125

trigger. Frank blessed that trait, for had the shots been better aimed they would have gone through the thorn fence like paper, it being only a screen, and not a solid wall. A moment later a score of natives burst from cover and made a rush across the open towards the camp, waving their spears and banging off their unaccustomed fire-arms.

Had the defenders not been prepared, the whole affair might have been over in a few seconds, for the attackers would have torn aside the thorn fence and been inside before anything could have been done to check them. As it was, they received a shock.

The instant the first natives burst from cover Frank opened fire, shooting with an accuracy born of long practice on game, and even Mansfield, though no great hand with a rifle, scored his hits. One after another those who led the rush crumpled and collapsed. For a moment the others wavered, and then, as a couple more rolled over on the trodden grass, they turned and fled back for the cover of the trees.

"That's given 'em something to think about!" Frank exclaimed, as he rammed a fresh clip of cartridges into his magazine. "That's something on account in return for those four runaway carriers they speared." He tried to speak calmly, though there was a tremor of excitement in his voice. He glanced at Mansfield, whose face had taken on a look of determination, though his hands were shaking slightly as he ejected the last cartridge.

"It has," Mansfield grunted, rubbing a shoulder that had been bruised by the unaccustomed recoil. "What's the next item on this infernal programme—do you think they'll try again?"

"Sure to, but not in the same way, I fancy, after the rap across the knuckles they've had." Frank turned and beckoned to Mawanza, who would be likely to know more about native tactics.

Mawanza expressed his opinon promptly. "They will not come again while the day lasts; they will sit in a circle round us, hidden by the trees, and watch that we do not escape. In the dark, when the masters cannot see to shoot, they will return and cut our throats. But," he added quite cheerfully, "my spear is sharp, and I will take some of these baboons-without-tails with me when I enter the land of the spirits."

Mawanza's estimate of the situation seemed to be correct. No second wild rush across the open materialised, and the only sign of the enemy lurking in the bush was the firing of an occasional shot that sang harmlessly high overhead.

Those within the boma had been far too keyed-up and busy since dawn to heed anything beyond their immediate surroundings, but now that the position had become temporarily one of stalemate, they became aware of other happenings that had so far passed unnoticed.

Not long after sunrise that morning an insignificant-looking cloud had appeared on the horizon, hardly visible owing to the universal heat haze. Rapidly it had increased in size, and by the time those in the camp noticed it, the rolling folds had filled the whole eastern sky. Where the sun caught them they shone white and dazzling, but beneath their colour was a peculiar shade of greenish black, varied at intervals with blotches of deep purple and of indigo, in and out of which the lightning flickered.

Frank touched Mansfield on the arm and pointed. "Look," he said, "the break of the rains."

Like scouts in front of an army, streamers of vapour moved in front of the advancing pall. They passed across the sun, obscuring it from sight, and bringing a hushed twilight to the earth beneath. Not a leaf rustled in the windless air, and even the endless humming and chirping of the insects in the undergrowth was stilled. The only sound was the menacing rumble of the thunder, each roll a little nearer and louder than the last.

The inky battalions rolled forward across the sky, and the world beneath lay silent and expectant.

Then another sound reached the ears of those who listened; it was the lashing of the forest before the gale. Steadily the roar became louder, while close on the heels of the wind moved a vast grey curtain hung between heaven and earth—the rain itself.

A vivid flash of blue-white lightning shot from the pall overhead, striking close to the camp and half-stunning its occupants with the splitting crack of its detonation. A second later the wind was on them, and, following Mawanza's example, Frank and Mansfield dropped to the ground to save themselves being blown off their feet.

It was lucky that they did so, for under the violent impact half the loose branches that formed the boma leaped into the air, joining the whirling cloud of dust and leaves that was tearing over and through the camp. Another flash and then another struck down in streams of dazzling light, their thunder-claps drowning for a moment even the noise of the wind. And then the grey wall of the rain reached the spot.

It did not fall in drops, but in solid rods of water, driven almost horizontally, from the force of the wind behind them. In a moment the parched ground was wet, then a-sheen, then almost ankle deep.

Soaked through instantly, Frank and his companions crouched beneath the downpour, while the rods of water hammered down upon their unprotected bodies,

and the deafening orchestra of the thunder crashed and
rolled.

Though the breath was almost beaten from him,
Frank's brain was working rapidly. He knew the effect
that torrential rain can have on natives caught in the
open; indeed, there was an example before him in
Mawanza and the man with the wounded shoulder. He
caught Mansfield by the arm and bawled in his ear:
"This is our chance?"

Frank and Mansfield staggered to their feet, picked up
their rifles, and crammed some spare ammunition into
their sodden pockets. Mawanza, awakened from his coma
by Frank's vigorous shaking, kicked his companion to
life and grabbed a bundle of tinned provisions and his
master's blankets. A moment later the four had passed
through one of the gaps that the wind had blown in the
fence, and were staggering and splashing across the
open ground towards the shelter of the surrounding
bush.

They reached it with grunts of relief, for the thrashing
branches overhead at least broke some of the force of the
downpour. Onward they plunged, the roar of the storm
drowning all sounds of their progress.

As they had already guessed, a cordon of watchers had
been posted round the camp; but at the moment not one
of them was functioning. Frank, leading the party as it
plunged forward among the trees, nearly stepped on one
of these sentries. The man was crouching behind a
sheltering trunk, his head between his knees and his
hands clasped above it in a futile attempt to fend off the
rain that poured in streams down his naked body. The
party passed him within a yard, but he did not raise his
head, for no inkling of the fugitives' presence had reached
his numbed senses.

They had put more than a mile between themselves and the abandoned camp when the wind began to drop and the rain to fall with less force. The thunder-rolls grew fainter. Though always violent, the first storm of the season is usually of short duration. Presently the rain ceased as if turned off with a tap, and blue sky appeared in the wake of the passing clouds.

Once more the sun shone down, but on a very different world. The air was no longer like warm cotton-wool to breathe; it was fresh and clean, and the heat haze had entirely vanished. Shadows, blurred for so many days, now lay sharp and black beneath the trees, whose every twig sparkled with rain-drops that the hot rays would soon absorb. After months of dryness, the unforgettable scent of the newly wet earth rose like incense, and everywhere the calls of beast and bird and insect gave thanks for the life-giving boon of the rain.

Mansfield, whose wet socks had begun to blister his feet, dropped a little behind. Having signed to Mawanza to take the lead, Frank joined him to urge him on.

"Now that the storm's over those natives surrounding the camp will wake up," he said, "but I don't suppose they'll start investigating to see if we're still there. They wouldn't think of starting out in a storm themselves, and so it wouldn't occur to them that we should do it. Still, it's just possible that some bright lad might notice that the place looks deserted, in which case they'll be after us in no time."

Mansfield nodded and caught up again, his shirt and shorts, like Frank's, steaming steadily under the rays of the sun, and his soggy pith-helmet slowly hardening into the weird shape it had assumed. "Where are we making for?" he asked.

"Home to mother," Frank replied facetiously.

"What do you mean?"—Mansfield managed a smile.

Frank felt there was no harm in talking as long as they spoke in low tones. "Taking the nearest way towards the Zambezi, and the southern side of the river, if we can get there. The outlook's none too bright, even when we've shaken off those natives behind. We've no stores except that bundle Mawanza grabbed; the rainy season is on us, and it's a long way to British territory and the civilised parts. Still, we'll make it somehow," he added with an assurance he did not feel.

"I suppose you're right," Mansfield admitted with a sigh, "but the whole business is absolutely sickening. If only those natives hadn't broken out as they did, and if only the rainy season hadn't arrived! We were on the verge of success, I'm certain, and would have made contact with my cousin in another few days. Now we're no better off than when we started."

"Yes, it's rotten luck, but it can't be helped," Frank agreed. "You'll just have to try again when the dry weather returns, in four or five months' time."

"But by then it may be too late," Mansfield growled. "By then my uncle's will may have passed probate, or whatever they call it, and once that concern has got its claws on to the money, it'll be the job of the world to make 'em disgorge."

Mentally Frank agreed, though he did not say so. He tried to put things in a more hopeful light, stressing the law's proverbial delays, so as to prevent Mansfield from getting despondent.

Meanwhile they trudged steadily onwards, keeping one ear cocked behind them for any sounds of pursuit.

Mawanza, now leading the party, was putting all his bush-craft into practice. He knew that after the rain which had fallen their spoor would be trebly easy to follow, for the heels of the white men's boots would print themselves deeply in the damp soil and remain until the next storm washed them out, which might not occur for hours. He took advantage of every stony patch where no marks would show, changing his course slightly as he crossed each one, so as to make the trail more difficult to locate again.

Afternoon passed into evening, and a suitable spot had to be found in which to spend the night. There was no moon, and clouds were drifting up which would hide the stars, making it impossible to continue moving in the pitch darkness.

At sunset they came on a low ridge that rose jagged and serrated, like the skeleton backbone of some vast prehistoric creature, and halted beneath an overhanging slab of rock. It was not an ideal spot, but at least it would provide some shelter in case the rain should come on again.

They dared not light a fire, for fires can be seen from far away, as Mac had already found out. However, the air was warm and their clothes were almost dry, and the tinned food they had with them could be eaten cold. As for the prowling beasts of the forest, they must trust to luck that none came that way.

As they sat, talking in low tones before rolling themselves in the blankets that Mawanza had snatched up, Mansfield mentioned the storekeeper whom Frank had visited and whose report had led them into their present predicament.

"I'd almost forgotten him," Frank admitted. "Now I come to think of it, we can't be very far from his place, striking, as we are, direct for the Zambezi."

He threw a word to Mawanza, and then went on:

"Yes, Mawanza says that if all goes well we shall pass

close to that store about noon to-morrow, and reach the Zambezi in the evening."

"Then if we pass close we'll call, and perhaps raise some more stores for the journey."

Frank grinned in the darkness. "You haven't seen the fellow yet, but I have, and judging by past experience, all we're likely to raise is a volley of abuse. All the same, we'll drop in, for I want to ask him what the deuce he meant by setting us on a false trail and nearly getting us done in. Living on the edge of the district, he must have known what conditions there were like."

"I don't think it was a false trail for a minute," Mansfield answered. "Oglethorpe's somewhere around, and this man Pieters probably knows a deal more than he told you. I mean to have the full dope out of him."

"You can try," Frank laughed, "but I doubt if you'll get it."

"Put me alongside him and you'll see!" Mansfield retorted confidently.

Frank did not reply; when Mansfield set eyes on the storekeeper he might not be so sure of success.

The night passed without any disturbance from either wild beasts or pursuing natives. Rain fell again about midnight, but not as heavily as the first storm; and though the spray blew in upon them, Frank was thankful for the downpour. It would wash out any spoor they had left behind. With the return of daylight the party pushed on again.

The hope that they had completely shaken off pursuit was doomed to disappointment. It was not long before they were aware of natives moving in the bush.

There were two courses open to them: to face round or continue pushing on. After a brief consultation they chose the latter, for the featureless bush offered no suitable spot for a stand. Also, as Mawanza urged, each step took them farther out of the area, and the enemy might be afraid to enter the sphere of other tribes.

The party hastened ahead, expecting attack at any moment. But none came. The unseen enemy seemed to be contenting themselves by throwing out flanking parties and shepherding the fugitives forward, refraining from molesting them as long as they kept to the path they were following. Even Mawanza, who knew the tactics of his own race, was puzzled.

"Perhaps they fear to close, knowing the masters' straight shooting. But if so, why do they not go back? But who can tell what these baboons-without-tails are thinking about?" he added with a snort of disgust.

At last Frank and his companions came in sight of the storekeeper's thatched buildings crowning their little rise, and at the same time they became aware of something else. The unseen enemies who had dogged them so persistently had quietly faded away, as though the task which they had set themselves was done.

CHAPTER FOURTEEN

THE MASK COMES OFF

AFTER telling Mawanza and the man with the cut shoulder to wait beside the track, Frank and Mansfield climbed the little rise and approached the store. They stood their rifles against the wall outside, and entered the dim interior that Frank had seen before. The same smell of trading-goods greeted him, and as his eyes became accustomed to the gloom, he saw once more the bearded and truculent figure of its occupant.

It was the man behind the rough counter who spoke first.

"So it's you back again, is it? I thought I told you I didn't want to see you this way again. And you've brought your pal, eh? But that won't stop me chucking you out again as I did before; I can handle two of you as easy as one."

Frank glanced at Mansfield to see how he was taking this form of greeting, and if, now he had come face to face with the man, he was still quite so confident of pumping him for information.

He found Mansfield leaning forward, staring at the speaker with an expression of dawning comprehension in his eyes.

"James!" he exclaimed. "You're James Oglethorpe!"

The other laughed.

"So my fine growth of beard doesn't hide my identity from a cousin's loving eyes," he sneered. "So you've run me down at last—more fool you; but then you always were a half-baked idiot about your own interests. Well, now you've done so, what about it?"

Mansfield seemed too taken aback by the discovery to make any reply, and even Frank had the wind taken out of his sails for a moment. The revelation explained several things that had been vaguely puzzling him. Remembering what he had heard from Mac, the first one leaped to his lips.

"If you're Oglethorpe, where on earth is Pieters who used to own this store?"

"Pieters? You'll find him round at the back if you care to look, under a neat little mound. I didn't bother to order a tombstone, complete with fittings," he added cynically; "he didn't strike me as the sort to have many virtues to inscribe upon it."

"Do you mean that you——" Frank began.

"If you're thinking I murdered him, you're wrong for once. I'd no need to. He was a pretty sick man—dying, in fact—when I got here. Malaria and drink combined. This proposition struck me as just what I wanted. So I stopped with him till he pegged out, planted him like a Christian, and stepped into his shoes. Got any comments to make?"

Frank had not. From what Mac had said about Pieters, the tale was probably true in every detail.

Meanwhile Mansfield had found his tongue.

"You call me a fool, James, for taking the trouble to come out all this way and find you, but you just listen to what I've got to tell you. I fancy you'll think differently then. You remember Uncle Henry? Well, he died six or seven months ago."

"I shan't go into mourning," Oglethorpe sneered.

"As you know, he was well off, and in his will he left his money to be equally divided between us. But he expressed it so badly that unless both of us were known to be alive at the time of his death, it all goes to one of those charity ramps that got on the soft side of him."

"Sort o' thing the old fool would do."

"Maybe, but don't you see the point? You'd vanished after that plane accident, and that concern is trying to have your death presumed, so as to scoop the lot. I was not convinced you were dead, and that's what's brought me out here. Think of it—now I've found you, there's £20,000 each in our pockets as soon as you reappear."

"So I'm to reappear, am I?" Oglethorpe retorted. "What sort of a mug do you take me for?"

"If you're thinking of what made you leave England so suddenly, you can take it from me that's all over." Mansfield went on. "A few days after you left, the police ceased thinking you were in any way responsible. They had come to the conclusion that your friend's fall on to the pavement from a fourth-storey window was entirely an accident."

Oglethorpe leaned back against the shelves behind him, and thrust his thumbs into his belt. "It seems to me I've heard all this fairy story before. Yes," he added, glancing at Frank, "you told it all to me nearly as nicely some weeks ago, I remember."

He swung round suddenly to Mansfield, sticking out his beard aggresively.

"Do you think you're going to catch me with that sort o' fly-paper? The London police aren't fools, I'll say that for them. Do you think I can't see through their game, and yours too? They know what happened all right, and they're lying low in the hope I'll stick my head out to have it hit!"

"Do you mean to say you really did throw that fellow out?" Mansfield ejaculated.

"You won't catch me like that," Oglethorpe retorted quickly, realising that he had let his tongue run away with him. "All I say is that I'm not such a mug as to reappear."

Mansfield seemed nonplussed. It had never occurred to him until this moment either that his cousin had really killed his shady friend, or that he would refuse to seize the chance of his share of the legacy. Meanwhile Frank remembered something that the discovery of the storekeeper's real identity had put out of his head—their original reason for turning aside to visit him.

"Look here," Frank began, "what you did in the past's not my business, but there's something else that is. When I was here last you advised me to go to Makabi's village and take your cousin with me, even mapping out a path that wouldn't bring us near this store again, lest Mansfield should recognise you, as he has done now."

Oglethorpe's only reply was an aggressive grunt.

"You sent us up there knowing the present attitude of the natives. Looks as if you had hopes they'd blot us both out, as they very nearly did," Frank went on grimly.

"How should I know anything about the attitude of niggers thirty miles away?" Oglethorpe retorted.

"Because—" A certainty flashed through Frank's brain. "Because you're the man who's been supplying them with modern rifles and stirring them up. I'll bet you rubbed your hands when you got that message from them saying we'd turned up there and asking what they should do. And we know what your reply was—but it didn't come off. Now then, what have you got to say to that?"

Oglethorpe let out a harsh bark of a laugh. "What have I got to say to that? Why, that it's a darned profitable business. I make two or three hundred per cent on the weapons supplied. Honest trade, for I don't cheat them, and they get the best. The only snag is that they don't seem to be able to hold 'em straight."

The whole sequence of the last few days fell into place in Frank's mind, even the reason why the natives had refrained from attacking when they found the party was making straight for the store. Oglethorpe being in command, they were leaving the final move to him.

"I see. Now we know what sort of a fellow you are, though it's a mystery to me why you wanted to do us in," Frank replied slowly. "If you hadn't sent us up there we should never have known about your dirty game at all, and anyway it's the business of the Portuguese Government, and not ours," Then with a sudden burst of anger Frank added, "You're a disgrace to your own colour! Faugh! you make me sick, you rotten swine!"

Frank fully expected another furious leap over the counter, and he was quite ready to meet it, but Oglethorpe merely grinned.

"Very well done," he sneered. "You'd make a fortune in any third-rate film where they like that sort of stuff."

Mansfield laid a hand on Frank's arm. "Come on, let's clear out. What are we wasting time for on him? I've got what I came for: I know now he's alive. If he doesn't want to come back to England, so much the better for decent people at home."

"Are you really going?" Oglethorpe asked in a tone of silky smoothness.

"Yes, we are!"

"Oh, no, you're not!" With a sudden movement Oglethorpe whipped his hand beneath the counter, and produced an automatic pistol of heavy calibre, and at the same moment with the other hand he jerked a string behind him which started a tinny bell jangling some-where outside. His eyes now blazed with temper in the way Frank had seen them on his previous visit.

Frank and Mansfield were unarmed, for they had, following the custom of the country, parked their weapons outside when they entered.

Frank saw that he had little chance of being able to grapple with the man, for Oglethorpe would put a bullet into him before he could surmount the intervening counter. There was less risk in a backward leap for the door and the rifles standing outside, but that would leave Mansfield a hostage to fate. He glanced round quickly for something to seize and throw, but there was nothing within reach. As he hesitated, the door behind him was suddenly darkened by half a dozen armed natives, who must have been waiting behind the building for the summons of the jangling bell.

It was Mansfield who spoke first. "What on earth are you playing at, James?" he demanded angrily. "Put that thing down at once!"

"I said you were a fool, shoving your fat head in where it wasn't wanted, didn't I?" Oglethorpe retorted. "I suppose you thought I was going to let you stroll off. If so you've got another think coming, besides what's coming to you now."

"If you imagine I'm going to run off to the Portuguese police with my tongue hanging out, you're wrong. If they catch you—which I sincerely hope they may—it won't be through me."

"Bad for the family honour, eh?" Oglethorpe sneered. "'Cousin blows the gaff on cousin' 'sort o' thing. But I wasn't thinking of that so much. No, I can see you trotting home like a virtuous little lad and saying nothing about the doings of the black sheep of the family except that he's alive. That wouldn't make them sit up and take notice at Scotland Yard, would it? Oh no!"

"But I've told you—"

"You can keep on telling till you break your jaw, but it makes no difference. James Oglethorpe has vanished, and as you two have been fools enough to find him, you're going to vanish too." He made an expressive gesture.

"Those people at Makabi's made a mess of things and didn't finish the job, but there won't be any mistake this time."

He waved the automatic to emphasise the point.

Faced with a crisis, Mansfield became suddenly quiet. "So you mean to add more murders to your record?"

"More? That gives you away, doesn't it? I thought you told me that affair in London was known to be an accident." Oglethorpe leaned suddenly across the counter, projecting his bearded chin. "I can see through you like a pane of glass; you're nothing but a coppers' nark, as I've thought all along. Murder you? Maybe I shall one day, but I won't spoil the pleasure of anticipation."

He made a sign to the natives crowding the doorway, and they closed in.

Frank made a shrewd estimate of what was passing in the speaker's mind. Though Oglethorpe might not have the slightest qualms about shooting them down then and there, he had a vein of cunning and caution in his make-up. Despite what had been said, he was convinced that the British police were using Mansfield and his story of a legacy to draw him into the open, and there was a possibility that, as a second string in case the first snapped, they might be following up behind somewhere. It would make things doubly awkward, on the top of his other lapses, if they arrived suddenly and discovered a couple of fresh graves behind the store. On the other hand, if he held these two in safe keeping, they might be turned to considerable advantage as hostages if the worst came to the worst.

"Now what's it to be?" Oglethorpe asked as his men closed in. "Going quietly, or shall I tell these natives to handle you as they'd like to do? You see this fellow?" —he pointed to one of them—"his brother was one of those you shot yesterday outside your camp. He'd pick a nice bone with you if I'd let him. Decided to accept the situation? That's good. Then you come along with me, and don't forget that at the first sign of foolishness I'll hand you over to these chaps!"

Oglethorpe led the way out of the store, past the spot where Frank and Mansfield had left their rifles, which of course had now vanished. They had expected to be taken to one of the buildings at the back, but instead their captor moved onwards towards the bush.

As he followed, Frank wondered what had happened to Mawanza, who had been left beside the path to await their return. Was he still there, or had he already been taken? Frank reflected that Mawanza was quite capable of looking after himself, and if he were on the alert he would not be easily taken. He dismissed from his mind, however, any hope of help from that quarter, for the odds were too great.

Turning his thoughts from Mawanza, Frank wondered where Mansfield and himself were being taken. Clearly to some spot deep in the bush. Surrounded by the natives, and with Oglethorpe tramping in front, they followed a definite beaten track between the trees.

Half a mile from the store they reached the base of a hill, and began to ascend its rocky side. About a third of the way up they reached a peculiar mound, a regular half-moon of stones over which trees and undergrowth had

Mansfield came down in the same fashion, bumping against the sides.

spread in profusion. It looked like the dump from an abandoned mine-shaft, and as Frank came closer he saw that this was indeed so, for in the middle of the arc of stones appeared the black mouth of the shaft itself.

"I happened to find this place a year or two ago," Oglethorpe remarked with cynical pleasantness. "Any idea what it is?"

"It looks like an ancient working," Frank replied calmly. He was not going to give Oglethorpe the satisfaction of seeing him either surly or apprehensive.

"Hit it first shot! One of the places where those early Portuguese mined for gold, and either they worked out the reef and abandoned it, or else they were killed off by the natives. Anyway, it's been lost for centuries. This hill's a regular honeycomb of galleries. I've found them useful the last few months, and they're going to come in very handy now."

He turned to give an order to those guarding the captives.

Three of them vanished behind some bushes and re-appeared dragging a roughly made windlass and stand, which they proceeded to erect over the mouth of the crumbling shaft. Having fixed it, they wound a length of wire rope on to the drum and hooked on a large iron bucket.

"It's come in nice and handy again, you see," Oglethorpe commented. "And now let me introduce you to your new home." He stabbed a finger downwards. "It's quite a palace down below, and you can get all the exercise you want exploring the workings. Sorry I can't rise to electric light, but I'll allow you a candle." He dropped his bantering tone and added sharply, "Get on with it—I haven't all day to waste!"

Frank gave a slight shrug to his shoulders, for resistance

was useless, and stepped to the lip of the shaft. He placed one foot in the bucket and grasped the wire rope above it. The natives at the windlass handles promptly began to lower him into the depths.

The bucket spun slowly round, and Frank fended himself away from the crumbling sides of the shaft with his free foot. He had no idea how deep the place was, and he was pleasantly surprised when he touched bottom only about twenty feet from the surface. He stepped out on to a mat of leaves and fallen rubbish, and the bucket was drawn up again.

Frank waited, leaning against the arch of rock that led into the dark interior of the hill. Against the ragged circle of sky above he could see Mansfield coming down in the same fashion, bumping against the crumbling sides and dislodging a shower of small stones. Once more the bucket descended with food, and rose again for the last time.

Oglethorpe's head appeared, a black knob against the clouds.

"Now you're as snug as a bug in a rug! Be good down there, and don't get into mischief. And if you think you've any chance of climbing out, just remember I'm leaving a couple of my men at the top with guns to blow your heads off. S'long!"

Frank and Mansfield heard the scrape of the portable windless being dragged away, followed by the sound of departing steps.

CHAPTER FIFTEEN

LANDSLIDE

THE two men at the bottom of the shaft looked at one another.

"Your cousin is right," Frank remarked with a twisted grin, "we've been a proper pair of fools and landed ourselves in a nice mess. Oh, it's myself I'm mainly blaming; I'd seen the fellow before, and ought to have been more on the lookout for squalls, even though I'd no idea he might be Oglethorpe."

Mansfield pushed back his misshapen helmet and ran his fingers through his carroty hair. "I still can hardly believe it. The surprise of recognising him behind that beard in the person of the trader you'd told me about was big enough, but his present attitude floors me completely. I'd have thought he'd have jumped at the chance of that money."

"Reckons the cash isn't worth a hemp necktie. He's taking no risks whatever, especially with his present law-breaking on top of the past. It's just our luck he didn't shoot us offhand; anyway, he's determined we shan't have a chance of becoming a danger to him."

Mansfield, however, had lost interest in what Frank was saying. He was looking round the gloomy hole, with its dark arch leading away into utter blackness. "We've got to get out somehow," he muttered.

"That's what the mouse says inside the wire trap before cook comes along and pops him in a bucket of water," Frank commented. "Meanwhile, let's have a look at the stuff he's left us. Things won't seem so bad when we've got something inside us. It must be past noon now, and we had our sketchy breakfast before dawn."

The contents of the bundle could hardly be called lavish, but still it was food. There was also a stoppered calabash of water and two or three candles, though Oglethorpe had either forgotten, or with sardonic humour omitted, to supply any matches. Luckily, however, Frank had a box in his pocket which was now fairly dry again after the soaking, and with care could be made to strike.

He lit one of the candles and stood it on a ledge just inside the arch, for the sky far overhead had become overcast again, and it was difficult to see what he was doing. Presently rain began to fall in sheets outside, the water descending the shaft in a whirl of drops and spray. The two moved into the shelter of the passage, taking their bundle with them.

Having eaten, Frank suggested that they should explore farther. Mansfield nodded agreement; he was not interested in the old working, but it would be something to do, and better than sitting about brooding.

They took a candle each and penetrated deeper into the tunnel. Almost at once they came on a litter of broken boxes, some long and others small and square. Oglethorpe had said that the place had proved of use to him in the past, and the reason was now obvious, for as the stencil marks showed, the cases had once held rifles and ammunition. It had been his store from which he had been supplying the disaffected natives with arms.

Mansfield glanced at the splintered wood with some interest. "Plenty of fuel here," he said; "we could make ourselves a fire to cheer things up a bit."

"Yes, and be choked by the smoke," Frank replied, shaking his head. "Our only air comes down the shaft, and if we turn that into a chimney we'll be suffocated."

Mansfield had to admit the force of the argument, and the two turned away and pushed on deeper into the workings.

The tunnels trended upwards, not downwards, following the twists and turns of the gold-bearing ore. At several places branches led away into the darkness beyond the glimmer of the candles, a glimmer that was progressively becoming more feeble as the flames shrank to pin-points.

"We'd be fools to try going any farther," said Frank. "There's no ventilation beyond what comes down the shaft, and deeper in the air must be absolutely foul."

The two retraced their steps, and the candle-flames once more rose on their wicks and assumed their normal size.

Not far from the entrance to the main tunnel, and close to where the broken boxes lay, they found a piece of smooth dry floor, and threw themselves down to rest, blowing out the candles, realising the necessity of saving them as much as possible.

A faint twilight, mingled with spray and damp air, filtered in upon them from the bottom of the shaft, for it was still raining heavily outside, and showed no signs of stopping. But their chosen spot was warm and dry, thanks to the upward trend of the workings and the solid rock of the hill that formed their roof.

The hours dragged slowly past. At length the outline of the arch began to fade, and they knew that the sun was setting. Frank lighted one of the candles again, and idly watched its flame rising straight and steady, for deep in the hill there was not the faintest draught to make it waver. Frank was later to remember with thankfulness that he had noted that apparently trivial fact.

They ate some more food, washing it down with a drink each from the calabash. They blew out the candle and settled themselves as comfortably as they could for the night, lulled to sleep by the murmur of the rain that was still falling with relentless violence on the world outside.

It was about four o'clock in the morning that Frank and Mansfield were suddenly awakened. The air was filled with a low rumbling noise. At first Frank thought it was the echoes of thunder outside, but it had not the right note. It was a duller sound altogether and more prolonged, and as he sat up in the pitch darkness, he was certain he could feel the solid hill tremble about him.

"What's that?" came Mansfield's voice out of the blackness.

"Don't know. Something's happened." Frank struck a match and lit the candle that had been stuck, in a dab of its own grease, on a handy bit of rock. As the flame burned up they looked around, but could see nothing in any way different from what it had been when they lay down.

Sitting up, they listened, but the noise had died away, and did not return. Frank became aware that he could no longer hear the persistent rain outside, so it must either have turned into a drizzle or stopped altogether.

"Don't see anything wrong," Mansfield remarked as he sank back again. "I thought for the moment that the whole hill was settling down on top of us—melting in the rain like an iceberg or something."

The words gave Frank a clue. Quite possibly the torrential rain after the long dry season had loosened the side of the hill somewhere, causing a landslip down its steep face; in fact, now he came to think of it, it would be just the sort of thing to produce that long rumble and faint tremor. He remarked as much to Mansfield and prepared to lie down again and finish his night's sleep. He turned over on his elbow to blow out the candle.

It was then that he saw something that made him pause.

On the previous evening he had idly noticed that the candle had burned with a perfectly upright flame. But now it was bent over at an angle pointing towards the maze of passages inside the hill, and a wisp of black smoke trailed and flickered beyond its elongated tip. There was a definite draught. Yet how could there be such a thing? To form a draught there must be two openings, yet the foul air that had driven them back from the inner tunnels showed clearly that there could be no such thing.

Frank looked at the candle in a puzzled way for a moment and then sprang up, pulling Mansfield to his feet. He seized the candle and held it aloft. Like a pointing finger, the flame still leaned inwards, away from the arch at the foot of the crumbling shaft.

The two pressed on along the sloping tunnels that led upward into the heart of the hill. Whenever they reached a junction they halted, anxiously watching the reactions of the flame. If it stood upright they retreated and tried again, waiting for it to turn horizontal like a sign-post and guide the way. Deeper yet they penetrated, into tunnels untrodden for centuries; but though the air was close and unpleasant, it was never too foul to breathe as long as they followed their pilot.

"We must be pretty near right through the hill," Mansfield muttered as he picked himself up after a stumble over some chunks of stone fallen from the roof.

Frank did not answer; he was far too much occupied with something he had seen. Out of the blackness above and in front of him gleamed a small bright light. He tried to tell himself it was only the reflection of the candle on some shiny facet of quartz, but it seemed to him to look like the luminous eye of some subterranean monster.

Shaking back an odd chill of fear, he took another step forward.

Instantly three or four other "eyes" appeared beside the first. With a start, Frank realised that he was no longer looking up at the rocky roof, but at a ragged hole beyond which the stars were shining after the passing of the clouds.

Frank's first instinct was to shade the candle, knowing how far a gleam of light can be seen. Together he and Mansfield peered up at the broken roof. It was as they had conjectured: the tunnel they were in, running not far from the outer face of the hill, had been breached by the rocks and soil that had slithered and rumbled down from the crest.

There was the opening, a slanting gash in the roof of the tunnel, but even by mounting on the pile of rocks that had crashed to the floor it was impossible to reach its lower lip. Nor could they build up the fallen debris into a higher mound, for the combined strength of both could not move the massive slabs.

"What about those long wooden cases you wanted to make a fire with," Frank suggested. "If we brought a couple and piled them on end we might do the trick."

The two men hastened back along the passages and presently returned with the boxes.

It was difficult to balance them on the top of the debris, but with Frank steadying them, Mansfield managed to climb up and grasp the lower edge of the hole.

It promptly broke away with a roar of stones and earth, making both men curse under their breaths at the noise. Mansfield tried again, and this time grasped something firmer. With a struggle he clawed himself forward up the sloping side of the hole, and reached the hillside above.

Frank found his a more difficult task, for he had nobody

to steady the boxes. However, just as they began to topple over he managed to grab the same projection that had helped his companion, and caught at the hand outstretched from above. A moment later he also was safely out.

The first pale streaks of dawn were beginning to appear. The night was over, and there was no time to waste.

Their next job was to get clear of the path of the landslide, for where it had passed lay a welter of slime and stones and broken trees that might at any moment slither farther down. Keeping parallel with the hillside, they scrambled for the undamaged slopes, and then descended to the more level ground beneath.

"Which way now?" Mansfield whispered.

Frank glanced at the sky, taking a bearing by the stars and the faint pallor in the east.

"This way," he said, pointing. "We must make for the Zambezi and get across it if we can before anyone discovers we've made our getaway. The river's not more than six miles away, I remember."

Moving as silently as possible, they slipped away among the trees, and with each step progress became easier as the wan light of the dawn increased.

"Hsst!" Frank held up a warning hand and paused, listening intently and peering back along the way they had come.

Yes, something was following them. He could hear the faint pad of bare feet and the rustle of branches as a moving body pushed them aside. Somehow their escape must have been detected, and one of Oglethorpe's armed natives was already on their track.

Being without any kind of weapon, Frank felt singularly naked and defenceless. He glanced round, and spotted a stout piece of deadwood lying at his feet. He picked it up, while Mansfield seized a loose stone. The two then stepped quietly aside behind the screen of a thick mass of undergrowth.

In the half light they saw a figure emerge from the shadows. Frank raised his club, ready to spring forward, and Mansfield swung back his stone.

"Master, is that you?" The whisper reached their ears, and there was no mistaking Mawanza's deep voice.

"Mawanza! What on earth brings you here?"

With a grin, a gleam of white teeth split the half-seen face. "I heard men moving, and the feet had boots. As the man-who-sells at the store is no doubt still asleep, I knew it must be you, for who else would have boots?"

"But how did you come to be here?" Frank asked.

Mawanza grinned again, and briefly told of his adventures. After waiting, as he had been told to do, beside the path, he had seen Frank and Mansfield leave the store under the escort of Oglethorpe and his men, and knew that something had gone very wrong. He had followed at a discreet distance, and presently, as the party returned from the top of the shaft, he had waylaid a straggler.

"He was cheeky and obstinate, but I made him speak," Mawanza went on, evading details of how it was done. He patted his spear, which Frank saw now bore ominous smears of crimson and added, "I then made sure he should not tell of having met me. I then went to the top of the hole, but could do nothing, for men with guns guarded it. So I hid in the bush and waited—and here I am."

Frank murmured a few words of appreciation to their faithful follower, and asked about the man with the cut shoulder who had been with him.

Mawanza gave a scornful grunt. "He ran away, abandoning the load I left in his charge. No doubt he has already met the fate of those hyena-men who deserted from the camp at Makabi's; but if he gets home to his village he will face a worse end from the spells of the Keeper of the Spirits whose orders he has disobeyed."

During the whispered conversation the three continued to push onward through the trees, making in the direction of the Zambezi. The daylight increased rapidly as the sun rose in a clear sky that for the moment was free of clouds.

The whole world sparkled and glittered from the previous night's downpour, and though only a couple of days had passed since the break of the rains, everywhere there were signs of the forest waking to life after the long dry season. Leaf-buds were bursting open on every tree, the green shoots of grass beneath them were sprouting almost visibly, and birds long silent were making the bush noisy with their varied calls.

The fugitives took no trouble to try to conceal their spoor; indeed, it was almost impossible to do so on that soggy ground. It was speed only that mattered, and the need to get on the other side of the great river before those behind became aware of their escape.

CHAPTER SIXTEEN

DEEP WATERS

IT was just a piece of sheer bad luck. They had encountered a strip of cultivated land, a tail running out from the main gardens of a hidden village, and to go round would entail a considerable detour. Frank reckoned that they were quite safe from being seen as they cut across the narrow strip of ground, for natives seldom come down to their fields so early in the morning. But he had forgotten that, owing to the break of the rains, the local people would be eager to get ahead with their planting, and that the usual routine would be broken.

Half-way across the open they saw something that a tongue of trees had so far hidden. A dozen women and several men were busy putting in seeds.

Frank and his companions reached the other side and the cover of the trees once more, but not before the sowers had caught sight of them and straightened their backs to stare.

"That's torn it!" Frank muttered to Mansfield. "It won't be long now before Oglethorpe gets wind of where we've gone. There they go," he added, as a high-pitched call came to their ears, to be answered by another, far away but still quite distinct. "In a few minutes Oglethorpe will be on our trail."

Half-walking and half-running, they hastened on, making for the tiny group of huts on the bank of the Zambezi where Frank and Mawanza had slept the night as they returned from their previous visit to the store.

They reached the place to find it deserted. With the break of the rains the natives had moved inland, probably to join the very people whom they had just encountered, and not a single canoe lay moored against the bank below the huts.

It was an unexpected blow, and a very serious one. The river was far too wide to be able to attract the attention of those who lived on the opposite bank, while the chance of intercepting a passing vessel was remote, for every fisherman would now be busy in his garden.

"Their canoes must be hidden somewhere," said Frank. "They can't have taken them with them."

"We must search along the bank, master," Mawanza put in. "They would hide them where no man would be likely to come on them by chance, dragging them high above the rising water and covering them from sight with branches and reeds. Such a place as yonder." He pointed downstream to where a belt of reeds backed by dense forest was visible two or three hundred yards away.

The three made their way in that direction and began their search, looking only in places where the bank sloped and up which it would be possible to drag a heavy dug-out. The forest was terribly dense, and a hidden canoe would almost have to be stumbled over before it was found. The reeds below were a maze of hippo paths, so that crushed and broken stems were no indication of anything having been hauled through them.

Slowly they worked their way along, examining every possible spot, and listening anxiously for any sounds of pursuit.

Presently they heard what they had been dreading—the voices of natives calling to each other, with Ogle-thorpe's shout chiming in at intervals. Their enemy had wasted no time.

The situation began to look desperate. A cordon was being formed and was slowly closing in on them, and soon it would pin them against the impassable barrier of the broad river. There was little chance of being able to hide, despite the thickness of the bush and the reeds, for Oglethorpe would certainly not be satisfied until he and his people had quartered every square yard.

And then at last, when Frank and Mansfield were beginning to give up all hope, Mawanza stumbled over a hidden dug-out.

It was small and old, but at least it looked as if it would float, and a couple of paddles were tucked underneath it.

With desperate haste they tossed aside the camouflage of reeds and branches. Mawanza seized the bow, and Frank and Mansfield gripped the gunwales, and they began to drag it down towards the river.

Despite its small size, it seemed incredibly hard to shift; to their anxious minds each second was as long as a minute, and they could hear the cordon steadily closing in. But at last the nose of the boat took the water. The three scrambled in, and thrust her out from the bank.

It had looked a cranky enough craft ashore, but after it had been launched it seemed ten times worse. For one thing, the trunk from which it had been cut had not been straight, and, for another, the hull was full of small cracks, caused by age and the hot sun, through which the water promptly began to dribble.

Frank seized one paddle, and Mawanza the other, and trying to avoid any undue noise or splashing, they widened the gap between themselves and the bank.

Things had been uncomfortable enough in the forest, but to Frank they seemed a great deal worse out on the river. Among the trees they had at least been hidden, but on the wide Zambezi they would be as visible as an ink-blot on a white tablecloth. The first person to reach the bank would see them instantly, and they would provide a perfect target for a well-aimed bullet.

There were only two paddles, and Frank and Mawanza had them, but there was plenty of other work for Mansfield to do. Already the bottom of the canoe was awash owing to the many spouting cracks. There was nothing to bale with, but by scooping rapidly with his hands, Mansfield managed more or less to keep pace with the inflow.

As the rains had only just started, the river had not yet had time to rise more than a few inches, but already the current was noticeably stronger. It was impossible to steer the cranky craft directly across, but a diagonal course would have the desired result, even though the opposite bank would be reached some distance downstream from the point of departure.

Every moment they expected to be spotted, and Frank and Mawanza bent to their paddles with a will. Every yard gained was valuable. At last, when they were quite half-way across the broad river, they heard a distant shout. Coming faster than the report, a bullet splashed up the water close by, followed by the sound of the rifle-shot.

It was the first of many, for Oglethorpe's armed natives had joined him on the bank, each one letting off his weapon with gusto. Had their target been closer it would have been safe enough, for the bullets would have sailed over it; but the much longer range neutralised the natives' passion for shooting high, and the splashes in the water were unpleasantly close.

Nor did all the missiles expend their force on the river. As the moments passed, first one and then another struck the canoe with dull thuds, making neat round holes

Mercifully no one in the dug-out was hit by the bullets.

through which the water spouted gleefully. Mansfield worked energetically at his baling, but the inflow became so rapid that he could not keep pace with it.

Mercifully none of the three in the dug-out was hit, though there were some close shaves. One bullet ripped the brim of Frank's sun-helmet, and another slicked through the tail of Mawanza's loin cloth. But these near misses were hardly noticed at the time, for they were too occupied in their efforts to keep the vessel moving.

Frank glanced towards the shore they were striving to reach. They were three-quarters of the way across now, and less than a couple of hundred yards remained to be traversed. But already the canoe was water-logged and in a sinking condition.

"She won't last much longer!" Frank cried to Mansfield. "We shall have to swim for it!"

"Wish I could, but I can't!" Mansfield shouted back.

With a start Frank remembered the time when he had gone in to pull the old witch-doctor out of the sombre pool among the hills, and Mansfield's exclamation that he would come too if he could, but that he couldn't swim. "I'll tow you, then," he called back, "though for heaven's sake lie quiet and don't clutch at me when I do so, or we'll both go under and drown."

The words were hardly out of Frank's mouth when the end came. The gunwale dipped beneath the surface and the riddled dug-out turned slowly over, depositing its occupants gently but deliberately in the water.

Like the others, Frank went under, but a moment later his head was above the surface again. A couple of strokes took him to Mansfield, and as he got his grip another thought struck him that sent cold shivers down his back.

The Zambezi swarms with hungry crocodiles, eager to

seize any living creature that comes within reach of their terrible jaws. Frank's hope of reaching the shore almost vanished, for the chances were ten to one that they would never do so. At any moment the horrible end might come. Grimly he struggled on, towing Mansfield with him, every nerve taut with apprehension. Meanwhile the bullets from the distant rifles smacked the water around.

Suddenly Frank recollected Mawanza, and turned his head to see what had happened to him. Mawanza would also be unable to swim, for in a country where every sheet of water is haunted by crocodiles, natives have no chance of learning even the rudiments of the art.

But as Mawanza had shown before, he was well able to take care of himself, however strange the circumstances. As soon as he had found himself in the water he had grabbed at the keel of the canoe, which, being of wood, still floated half-submerged. Supporting himself with one hand, he thrashed at the water with the paddle he still gripped in the other, looking like a tiny tug trying to tow the *Queen Elizabeth* along with it.

Frank saw that he could give no aid at the moment. The faithful follower must hang on until he could deposit Mansfield on the bank and swim out again.

Something bumped against Frank's legs, and he almost cried out, for his mind was full of crocodiles. But to his vast relief he discovered that what he had struck was a submerged sandbank. He let his feet drop and stood up, pulling Mansfield with him. Waist-deep, the two plunged forward, gaining several yards. Then the sandbank dropped away into deep water again; but now the goal was close. In another minute they had reached it safely.

Panting, Frank let go of Mansfield, and braced his nerves to face the peril of the river once more. At first he could not see Mawanza, and thought that he must be gone, but a moment later he caught sight of him some distance downstream.

Mawanza had not been wasting his time. Though the current had drifted him relentlessly away from the others, he was still vigorously splashing in his efforts to tow himself and his cumbrous support shorewards. Frank hurried along the bank, meaning to take to the water well downstream, and make as short as possible the distance he would have to swim.

But there was no need for him to plunge in. Just as he was about to do so, the upper half of Mawanza's body rose suddenly out of the river—he too had struck a hidden sandbank. He let go of his water-logged support, and shouting and waving the paddle he still held, he splashed his way forward. At this point no deep channel intervened, and a few seconds later he also had reached safety. At that moment Mansfield joined them, and the three scrambled up the slope and into the cover of the forest, where they threw themselves down for a brief but much-needed rest.

Frank could still hardly believe their good fortune, for he had been so certain that once the canoe had sunk they had little hope of reaching safety. As he squeezed the water from his clothing he commented to Mansfield on their strange immunity from seizure by crocodiles, and repeated the remark in the local tongue to Mawanza.

"It was the water we had to fear, not the evil beasts," the native replied in his deep voice. "I knew they would never come to drag us down."

"What on earth makes you say that? You know the Zambezi well enough. Why, even a man leaning from the bank to draw water has to be quick and wary lest he should be pulled in and never seen again."

A grin split Mawanza's black face. "Those men who fired guns at us hoped to strike us, but though a few hit the canoe and made it sink, most of the bullets struck their hard blows on the river. Crocodiles love silence, and they would feel those heavy slaps on the water and hasten away quickly."

Mawanza was perfectly correct, and Frank wondered why he had not guessed the obvious solution himself. Of course the firing would have scared all the crocodiles from the vicinity. The humour of the situation struck him, and he laughed; how wild Oglethorpe would be if he knew that his efforts to kill them had in effect saved their lives! He laughed again, and rose to his feet.

"Come on, Mansfield, this won't do. We've put the river between us and that undesirable cousin of yours, but that doesn't necessarily mean that he'll give up. Besides, we'll be hungry soon, and unless we find a village and raise food somehow, we'll starve. We're down to bed-rock this time and no mistake; even our only weapon, Mawanza's spear, went to the bottom when the canoe overturned."

Meanwhile, what of Oglethorpe on the other side of the river?

When he had burst through the trees and caught sight of the canoe and its occupants, he gave an angry exclamation, for he had felt certain of trapping them against the bank of the river. But they were by no means yet out of his reach. He gave a shout to call in his widespread cordon of natives, and opened fire himself with the rifle he carried.

Shooting across a wide sheet of water is always a tricky job, and he could not be sure of the range. His followers joined in, but the dug-out still made progress, growing smaller every minute. And then he gave a cry of joy as he saw the vessel disappear, leaving three tiny dots which he knew to be the heads of its crew.

He shouted to his natives to keep up their fusillade, while he himself shaded his eyes against the sun and the glitter from the river, eagerly hoping to see those heads disappear. Though the distance was great the atmosphere was clear, and he let out a violent oath as he saw the tiny figures emerge from the water and vanish into the green ribbon beyond it.

He turned savagely on his followers. "Stop shooting, you bungling fools! What's the good of supplying muck like you with rifles when you never hit anything you aim at? Find another canoe! Get a move on!" He let drive with another burst of swearing and waved his weapon threateningly.

The natives promptly scattered to obey his orders, lest in his rage he should back them up with a shot or two. But search as they would, they could not stumble on another dug-out. It was hours before at last they secured one, for they had to send a member of the party several miles inland to fetch a fisherman who could tell them where the rest of the local vessels had been secreted.

While Oglethorpe cursed his followers and kept them searching in every possible and impossible place, Frank and his companions pushed forward, leaving behind them the dense jungle and reed-beds that fringed the river area, and traversing the less-tangled forest that clothed the higher ground.

There were game paths everywhere, but except for the convenience they afforded to progress, they were of no use to them. What they were seeking was a native track bearing the recent spoor of feet, which would lead them eventually to some village deep in the bush.

At last they struck a track of the kind they were looking

for. It was far less clearly defined than the many game paths, and had it not been for Mawanza's sharp eyes they would have missed it altogether. It bore on its damp surface the impressions of bare feet; a couple of natives had passed along it since the previous night's rain, going in more or less the same direction that Frank and his companions had been tramping.

In single file they followed, Mawanza leading the way, with his eyes continually glancing down at the faint path to make sure that he was keeping the spoor. For five or six miles they trailed their unknown guides, and at last they reached the bank of a sandy river-bed. On the opposite side, against the background of trees and branches, appeared a small group of conical huts.

CHAPTER SEVENTEEN

AN OLD FRIEND REAPPEARS

It was a tiny place, only half a dozen huts altogether, but at least there should be a chance of obtaining something to eat. Frank and Mansfield sat down on a fallen log on the fringe of the little clearing, while Mawanza went to see what he could scrounge in the way of food.

Being so small, the place had no proper headman, but presently Mawanza returned with a depressed-looking savage and a couple of women bearing wooden bowls of coarse porridge. It was the best they could offer, and Frank accepted it with gratitude, wishing that he could give something in the way of exchange. But unlike the more rapacious headmen nearer civilisation, the old man did not seem to expect anything; it was customary for natives passing through to be offered anything they had, and the fact that these men were white did not affect the matter at all.

While the two ate the stiff porridge with their fingers, native fashion, Mawanza vanished again among the huts to glean what information he could from the local people. It was not long before he returned, and a glance at his face showed that he had got hold of something of interest.

"These people say," he began, "that there is a white man camped at a village three hours march from here." He pointed. "Those two whose spoor we were following told the women when they passed through, for they were on their way to the place where he is, to buy beads for their wives. They say he is one who often comes to these parts, bringing white men's things to exchange for produce."

Frank and Mansfield glanced at each other, the same thought in their minds.

"Did they tell you anything more about him?" Frank asked.

"No, master, but I can guess. Doubtless he is the hunter of elephants back here again, collecting the big teeth that he buried lest the police should seize them."

Clearly Mac's stratagem was no secret from the natives, though the Portuguese police had never learned it.

Frank nodded. Since their parting in Tete there had been plenty of time for Mac to collect a stock of trading goods and return to the district in the guise of a licensed hawker. "Then we'd better push ahead to that village right away," he said.

"Yes, master; the way is easy to find, they say, for we must follow the path that enters the trees beyond the huts, and we should be there before darkness falls."

Mawanza was right. Though the trail was faint, they found no difficulty in keeping it, and in the light of an angry sunset that threatened heavy rain they reached their destination. The inhabitants, busy with their evening tasks, looked up in surprise as they appeared, but in response to Frank's question they pointed to an erection of poles and thatch that had been run up on the outskirts of the village.

At the sound of the steps a tousled head appeared at the opening which served as a doorway. It was Mac, sure enough, and recognition instantly changed his guarded expression to one of welcome.

"Losh! if it's no' the pair o' ye back again! And that big native o' yours too! Well, well, who'd hae thought it? Where's your carriers and loads—behind?" He caught sight of his visitors' bedraggled clothing, which bore liberal signs of the rain, the river, and the grime of the tunnels. "Ye're no' looking so smart as ye were. But come in and sit ye down."

They entered the little shack which Mac's servants had run up as his temporary quarters. The interior was piled with his stock-in-trade, but an open space had been left in the middle to serve as a living-room. Though rough, the roof was well thatched and weather-tight, and it looked a haven of refuge to Frank and Mansfield after their recent experiences.

"And how hae ye fared since last we foregathered?" Mac went on, after pulling forward a couple of bales as seats and shouting orders to the cook-boy about the evening meal. "Did ye find yon fella ye was looking for?"

"We did," Frank replied with a short laugh. "In fact, in my case, I found him a second time, for I'd seen him before behind the counter of that store."

"Do ye mean it was Pieters? But that canna be—why, I've kenned Pieters the last ten year, and ye told me—"

Frank laughed again. "No, not Pieters; there was nothing left of him but a mound at the back of the store. You were right when you said he was a dying man when you met him last. It was his successor that I found— both times—and the second encounter was even more unpleasant than the first. But I'd better tell you the yarn from the time we parted."

Frank went on to give an account of their adventures, Mansfield putting in an occasional word. As he spoke, the rain which had been threatening began to fall, drumming steadily on the earth outside, and the thunder growled and rumbled through the gathering darkness. But within the shelter it was cosy enough, even though their light was only a smoky hurricane lantern that Mac's cook had placed among the tin plates when he had brought in the meal.

"Well, I never did!" Mac grinned, when Frank had brought his tale up to the present. "I was beginning to think that this country was getting ower-ceevilised for the likes o' me, but after I'm hearing all ye've been doing I'm no' so sure. I've heard tell o' trouble brewing among the natives beyond the river; so this swab's at the bottom o' that, eh? If it wasn't that I canna bide the police, I'd be o' a mind to tell them."

"It would pay you to send a runner to them with the straight tip," Frank grinned. "You'd put yourself in their good books for once, which might come in useful later."

"Aye, maybe ye're right. I'll think on it." Mac ruminated over the novel idea for a minute or two, and then continued. "And what might you two be planing?"

"Get back to British territory and civilisation and lawyers, to settle the matter of that will," Mansfield answered promptly. "Though things have turned out differently from what I expected, the result's the same. I've discovered that my cousin is alive, and I've done what I set out to do."

"Man, ye've done just nothing, nothing at all," said Mac, shaking his head solemnly. "What were ye reckoning for to do? Go and tell them ye've seen your cousin? They'd no' believe that; they'd want proof."

"I've got my witness," Mansfield retorted, indicating Frank.

"Him? He's no more use to ye than a bent penny to a slot machine." Mac leaned forward and tapped Mansfield on the knee with a thick forefinger. "He's your paid employee. They'd tak' no note o' him; they'd just say he was earning his money. They're canny folk, London lawyers—nigh as canny as us Scots. Maybe they'll speak to ye mortal polite, but they'll ask ye to produce either the man himself or an independent witness."

The probability that Mac was absolutely correct struck home, and Mansfield gave an exclamation of annoyance and chagrin." That'll mean I shall have to start all over again, and I don't know how much time I've still got in hand."

Mac grunted sympathetically. "'Tis verra aggravatin', but ye must face facts. There's naught ye can do now, with all your stores and carriers gone, and the rains turning the country into a bog, whiles. It'll no' be till next April-May that she'll start drying up again, nigh on six months yet. So ye'd best return to British territory— if ye're no' stopped on the way," he added significantly.

"Stopped? Who by?" Mansfield demanded.

Mac gave a snort at the other's obtuseness.

"After what ye've told me about yon cousin of yours, I canna see him just giving up as a bad job when he found you'd crossed the Zambezi. If he means to make sure ye'll no' get away to tell on him, that bit o' water'll no' stop him, I'm thinking."

Frank nodded agreement. While Mac had been speaking, his thoughts had turned in the same direction.

"Mind ye," Mac went on, "I'm no' saying he'll try and grip ye here, or in any village, for that matter. The people here belong to a different clan from those yonder, and he'll be scairt o' crossing them and maybe coming to blows. He's no' looking for a spear-blade inside him. But there's plenty o' places where he might succeed, for the bush is thick and the paths lonely between the villages. Though I'm no' wanting to get rid o' ye, I'm thinking ye'll be wise to be moving come the morn, afore he kens where ye are."

The advice was too sound to be ignored. Though had seen nothing of Oglethorpe since they had dived into the trees after escaping from the river, there was no knowing when he might come up with them again. But it was one thing to say that they would hasten on, and another thing to do it, for they were absolutely destitute of everything except the rags they stood up in.

Mac seemed to read Frank's thoughts.

"I canna gie ye much, for I'm no' so well supplied myself y'understand. But there'll be something for that native o' yours to carry in the way o' food, and a bolt o' cloth as well for trading at the villages as ye gang along. That'll see ye through, I shouldn't wonder."

"But we can't deprive you," Frank protested. "You can't have more stuff here than you need. We'll manage somehow."

"Havers! Do ye think I'm letting ye gang without a bite or a blanket for the journey? Besides, I owe it ye; did ye not help me when I was gripped by the police? If ye hadna got on the right side o' that commandant, it's in jail I'd be this very minute. Ye'll tak' what I gie ye and no argument!"

Frank and Mansfield began their thanks, but Mac cut them short.

"I've an old shotgun, too, ye can have. I canna spare ye a rifle, being only a puir wanderin' trader now who dinna need such things," he went on with a wink; "but the shotgun'll do ye fine for scaring off any wild beasties ye meet on the road. She makes a grand bang! And she'll come in useful whiles if ye want a guinea-fowl or a partridge for the pot."

The following morning broke damp and grey under

drifting clouds, though the rain of the previous night had ceased some hours previously. Frank and Mansfield said good-bye to their kindly friend and took the path that would lead them to the next village in the direction of the Rhodesian border. Calculating by the time taken on the outward journey to the same area, they reckoned, if all went well, to reach it on the second or perhaps the third day from now, crossing it somewhere close to where they had done so before.

Mawanza led the way, the bundle of necessities that Mac had generously supplied balanced on his woolly head, and in his hand he carried a spear that he had secured in some mysterious way from his hosts of the night before. Mansfield and Frank followed, the latter carrying Mac's aged shotgun over his shoulder.

The morning's march was uneventful. The clouds shredded into gaps through which the sun shone down, bringing out the colours of the bush—or rather the single colour, for everything was already green with burgeoning leaves and springing grass. Under the hot rays a faint steam rose from the earth, making the travellers feel that they were marching through some vast vapour-bath.

After a short midday halt they pushed on, reeling off a steady mileage. At this pace, Frank felt they should reach the border even more quickly than he had calculated. The afternoon passed and the sun began to sink towards the west, and they looked forward to reaching their destination for the night. Mawanza, who had been there before, said it was a large village, and added that as the headman was a friend of his there would be no difficulty in getting anything they wanted.

Suddenly Mawanza halted, holding up his hand for silence and listening intently. His ears, trained to interpret bush sounds, had caught something that the white men's hearing had missed.

"What is it?" Frank whispered sharply.

"I heard a big buck crash away suddenly, as if something had scared it. Over there." He pointed to the right and a little behind them.

"What of it?" Frank asked. "Probably it was put up by the natives making for the same village as we are ourselves."

The suggestion did not satisfy Mawanza. He laid down his load, knelt, and pressed his ear to the damp earth. He sprang up again with a new light in his eyes.

"I can hear boots," he exclaimed, "as well as the slap of bare feet."

Frank's thoughts immediately leaped to Oglethorpe. But it could hardly be he. If Oglethorpe were anywhere, he would be following on their spoor, dead astern, and not approaching from an angle. Or had he made a shrewd guess at the direction they would take, and cut directly across from the now-distant Zambezi to cut them off?

"Come on, master, the village is close," Mawanza urged, picking up his load and spear. "He will not dare to come among the huts, for the people would leap at the excuse of a fight with those followers of his from beyond the river."

They hastened on, scrambling down a little donga that crossed their path, and up the other side. Those who were approaching unseen must have heard and diagnosed the sound of boots slipping on the stones, and broke into a run. As the three topped the crumbling bank, Oglethorpe and a handful of natives appeared suddenly on the side they had just vacated, thirty yards away.

Oglethorpe gave a shout of satisfaction. His rifle went up, and it was only owing to the fact that he was panting after his run that the bullet struck timber instead of flesh.

Frank, who had been bringing up the rear of the party, swung round. He had Mac's old shotgun in his hands. He let drive with both barrels, and as a startled yell came from the other side of the donga, he plunged into cover on the heels of Mansfield and Mawanza.

The pellets of "No. 5" that had struck Oglethorpe and a couple of his men had done hardly any damage, merely penetrating his clothes and the skin behind, but they had given him a considerable shock. He had been so confident that those whom he pursued were entirely unarmed—having come direct, he knew nothing of their encounter with Mac. He realised instantly the danger of too close contact until he could get them in reasonably open country, where he could use his rifle from beyond the range of their shotgun.

While he hesitated on the lip of the donga, cursing at the sting of the pellets and trying to find out what damage he had sustained, Frank and his companions hurried onwards, and a few minutes later reached the comparative safety of the village.

CHAPTER EIGHTEEN

HIDE AND SEEK

As they passed in among the huts the headman rose from where he had been squatting amid his elders under the village council-tree and came forward to receive his white visitors, bearing a small present of meal.

"We were expecting you, for we heard two gun-reports," he said after the formal greetings were over, thus explaining why the customary present was already prepared. "Shall I tell my men to go and bring in what you killed?"

"We have shot nothing," Frank answered.

The headman looked disappointed. He had been hoping for a windfall of meat on which he could gorge himself that evening.

"It was evil men, not beasts, that we fired at," put in Mawanza. "You should turn out your young men and drive them away—that is what my own chief would do in my village."

The headman looked slightly startled. He had no desire to be mixed up in a row, but as Mawanza gave him a brief but dramatic account of recent happenings, his face cleared somewhat.

"You are my guests," he said to Frank," and here you will be safe, for these men will not dare to enter my village and seek you. But if you leave—" He ended the sentence with a gesture, and went on to give orders that a new hut should be put at the disposal of his visitors, and water and firewood brought for their use.

Frank and Mansfield took up their quarters, and after they had eaten their evening meal, called to Mawanza. The events of the past few days had given Frank a high opinion of his capabilities, and before deciding on the plan for the future, he wanted to have his retainer's advice.

Mawanza's opinion was already formed—in fact it bubbled out of him as soon as the subject was mooted.

"We must stay here for a while, master. If we leave when the morning comes we shall fall into an ambush in the forest. I will speak again to the headman, and though he will not send out his young men with spears, no doubt he will agree that they should go and bring us news. Perhaps the evil white man and those with him will go away," he added hopefully, "for they will find no food here, and will have to lie in the open when it rains."

Though eager to push on, Frank and Mansfield saw that there was something to be said for Mawanza's suggestion. Though there seemed little likelihood of Oglethorpe throwing up the sponge without another effort, they would at least know what he was doing, and be able to plan accordingly when they did decide on a move.

It was not long before news began to come in, and with it a certain amount of grumbling amongst the natives. Men coming from other villages, with bundles of foodstuffs to exchange for other produce, had been stopped, relieved of their loads, and turned back. Worse still, the game-traps which the local people had set in the vicinity of their gardens were being consistently robbed, and the nooses, so laboriously made from aloe fibre, cut and destroyed. How, they murmured among themselves, were they to protect their newly-planted crops if there were nothing to check beasts from eating them down during the hours of darkness?

Oglethorpe's plan of campaign became rapidly apparent. He was not going to attempt an entry to the village and bring on a crisis; his plan was far more subtle. He meant to annoy the natives till they realised that their guests were thoroughly unwelcome, and make them go. Once he had got them out again and on some lonely path, his chance would come.

The atmosphere of discontent in the village increased, and even the headman, though a friend of Mawanza, hinted broadly to Frank and Mansfield that he preferred their room to their company. Mawanza fumed and blustered, but he could do nothing, for the villagers were solidly behind their chief.

That evening they discussed the situation.

"We've got to face it," Frank said. "We must shift, and the sooner the better, for delay's not going to do us a scrap of good, as far as I can see."

Mansfield nodded. "You're right. So what about it? Make an early start as soon as it's light to-morrow, and try to dodge that infernal cousin of mine?"

"Not to-morrow—to-night, when the darkness will help us. There's a moon now, so it won't be pitch black, and we'll be able to see well enough. I don't say we'll shake him off, but we may get a good start before he finds we're gone, and every mile we cover will get us nearer the Rhodesian border. Not that that in itself will be any help, but Oglethorpe may think twice before following us very far beyond it, out of what he considers to be the safety of Portuguese territory."

Except for telling Mawanza, they let out no hint of their intention, and just after midnight they crept silently away from the village.

The night was warm and damp, but it was not actually raining, and through the slowly drifting clouds sufficient moonlight filtered down to make it possible to move without stumbling. They drew clear of the huts and entered the trees, taking a narrow path that led in the right direction. The path might be watched, but it was essential to keep to it, for not only must it serve as their guide, but an attempt to thrust a way through untrodden bush would be far too noisy.

They had traversed nearly a couple of hundred yards when a low sound from in front came to their ears. Mawanza turned his head, and Frank saw the moonlight flash on his teeth as he grinned. Cautiously they crept towards the source of the sound, and came on the watcher whom Oglethorpe had posted beside the track. He lay fast asleep, and from his open mouth issued lusty snores.

Mawanza slowly raised his spear, and his intention was obvious, but Frank touched his arm and shook his head. It was not so much from compunction as from prudence. A corpse found when the relief arrived would tell its own tale, whereas if the man were left to his slumbers, their flight might not be discovered for a long time, especially if rain fell and obliterated any spoor on the path.

For the next half mile they moved with care, in case a second and more wakeful sentry should have been posted. But they saw none, nor did they run into any of those noose-traps that, since the beginning of the rains, the local people had been setting across likely tracks. Possibly there had been none, but more probably Oglethorpe's men had destroyed them already.

As soon as they were well clear of the vicinity of the village they pushed on rapidly. The clouds above were thinning, ceasing to veil the moon, and leaving wide gaps through which the stars shone down. Continually they heard rustlings and the thud of hooves as the beasts of the forest fled away before their approach. But of those

sounds they took no heed; it was from behind that
the danger might approach, but all lay silent in their
wake.

That herald of the dawn, the morning star, lifted itself
above the eastern horizon, and the darkness below it
presently changed to grey and then to primrose. The
clouds that remained took on an edging of pink, and at
length the sun sent its level rays of golden light across the
tree-tops.

The narrow path wound onwards, and as the travellers
rounded one of its many bends they beheld an unexpected
sight. Riding towards them, with all the recklessness of
the African, was a native on a bicycle.

From the first glance Frank summed him up. The
native's singlet and trousers, and the flashy cotton hand-
kerchief round his waist, all spoke of a time-expired worker
returning from some distant mine or farm or township.
The bicycle was brand new, and clearly he had invested
most of his accumulated wages in the machine. Riding
it along the level paths, and carrying it down hillsides
and over ravines, he was bringing it home to dazzle the
eyes of his savage relations, and be able to visit other
villages rapidly and in style.

Instead of saluting in native fashion, the man made a
clumsy attempt to raise his hat, and promptly fell off.
However, no harm was done, and after murmuring a
word of greeting, he passed the travellers and remounted.
He had hardly passed out of sight when a thought struck
Frank that made him utter an exclamation.

"Curse! On a bike that fellow will reach the village
we've come from in an hour or so, and probably he'll be
intercepted by Oglethorpe. He'll be sure to say that he's
seen us, and that will blow the gaff completely."

Mansfield shrugged. "Maybe, but we have a good start,

and Oglethorpe can hardly travel much faster than we're doing, or catch us up easily."

"Can't he!" Frank retorted. "You've forgotten the bike. He'll knock that fellow off it and pinch it for his his own use, and be after us full split. It'll be a heaven-sent gift to him."

"But his natives—they won't be able to keep up."

"He won't expect them to. He knows they can't shoot straight and aren't a lot of use. He'll come on alone after us with that rifle of his, and if he can get a decent chance of a shot at us, we're for it. Let's hope we don't have to cross any open ground, for he'll be shy of getting close to us in thick stuff, having already had a taste of this old shotgun of Mac's."

As they pushed ahead, Frank kept continually glancing over his shoulder, for he knew that there would now be no warning sound of footsteps, and soft rubber tyres are almost noiseless.

At length they encountered what Frank had been dreading—a treeless depression more than a hundred yards wide. The party hastened across it, and as they reached the other side a report rang out sharply behind them. Mansfield stopped with a sudden cry, clutching at his right forearm with his other hand, blood welling up between his fingers.

"Hit? Quick, into cover before he fires again!" Frank pulled Mansfield after him into safety behind the foliage. "I'll have a look at it in a minute, but we can't stop here." They plunged forward, and did not halt until they had reached the shelter of a dense belt of trees and under-growth.

"Now let's have a look at it."

Mansfield had been lucky, for the bullet had missed the bone, drilling a neat round hole through his forearm.

Frank tore strips from the roll of calico that Mac had put in Mawanza's bundle for trading purposes, and set to work at bandaging the wound, while Mawanza stood on guard, watchful and listening.

Meanwhile Oglethorpe had seen that his shot had taken effect, though he did not know the extent of the damage. He hoped that he had at least finished off one of them, and that only two remained. He loaded again, remounted his stolen bicycle and swiftly crossed the open ground. He gave a grunt of satisfaction as he caught sight of the blood on the path, and a trail leading aside from it. He dismounted, rested his bicycle against a tree, and followed.

Mawanza heard him, and drew Frank's attention with a low hiss. Frank once more picked up the shotgun that he had laid down while he bandaged Mansfield; but he could see nothing amid the foliage slowly waving in the breeze.

Suddenly he caught sight of Oglethorpe's head lifting itself over a bush to peer. He swung up his gun and fired, but he was a second too late. Oglethorpe had spotted the movement and promptly ducked, and the pellets tore harmlessly over him, bringing down a shower of twigs and leaves. Frank let drive with the other barrel just below where the head had vanished, but Oglethorpe had darted away out of danger. He meant to get them, but he was taking no risks himself.

A tense silence followed, broken only by the calls of birds and the hum of insects, while both sides considered the next move.

Frank realised that they could do no good by stopping where they were; getting on must be their first consideration. It would no longer be safe to use the path, for Oglethorpe with his bike had every advantage there;

they must take to the forest and push along as best they could.

From his lair Oglethorpe heard them moving, and abandoning the bicycle that was no longer of use, took up the trail. Had his natives been with him he would have had an easy task, for more than once the party had to cross open spaces; but his want of experience in following spoor delayed him, and he dropped behind.

The distance between pursuer and pursued increased as the hours passed. By nightfall Oglethorpe was more than a mile behind, and as darkness fell he could no longer see the spoor. He halted. He guessed, and rightly, that he would not lose much by waiting, for Frank and his companions had been on the move since the previous midnight, and would be forced to halt also and get a short sleep.

Moreover, he did not relish the idea of stumbling on their hiding-place unexpectedly. They would hear him coming and be roused and ready, and in the darkness his rifle would have no advantage, while the spreading blast of Frank's shotgun would be deadly at close range.

Despite the throb of his wound, Mansfield passed a fairly comfortable night, Frank and Mawanza taking it in turns to keep watch. As Oglethorpe was also resting, naturally they heard nothing of him, but as they were ignorant of the fact, they did not relax their vigilance. Also there was a persistent lion that kept grunting and rustling in the undergrowth not far away, and they dared light no fire or bang off a shot to scare it away, lest it should betray their position to the man behind.

With weary eyes they saw the daylight beginning to return, and drew themselves heavily to their legs once more.

Though they had not yet reached the frontier and the

area beyond it where Mawanza's home village was situated, they were getting into country that he knew slightly, which made things easier for them now that they had abandoned the guidance of the path. In consequence they were able to shape a better course, avoiding both dense tangles of jungle and patches of open ground like that which had so nearly proved disastrous the day before. Of Oglethorpe they heard nothing, though at intervals they paused for a moment to listen intently, and hope rose in their hearts that he must have lost their spoor altogether.

It was shortly before noon that they came upon it—an obelisk some five feet high built of rough stones held together with cement, and with a rusty iron spike project- ing from its apex. For a moment Frank could not think what it was—could it mark the grave of some forgotten pioneer? And then he opened his mouth for a shout of joy that caution instantly silenced, for he had realised that it was one of the widely-spaced boundary pillars set up many years ago by the Frontier Survey. With a lighter heart he reached it, gave it a welcoming slap with his hand, and the three strode past it into British territory once more.

CHAPTER NINETEEN

BRASS BUTTONS

"Over the border and not a sign of that infernal cousin of mine on our heels," said Mansfield, a tone of gratification in his weary voice. "I wonder if he'll risk crossing it?"

"He may," Frank replied. "We've heard nothing of him since yesterday, and it's possible he may have lost our trail and given up. Still, we can't take anything for granted."

Mansfield groaned. "I shan't be sorry when we strike some place where we can have a bit of a rest. Jogging on eternally isn't all jam, with this arm of mine."

Frank glanced anxiously at his companion. The way Mansfield had stuck it had been magnificent, and he was certainly a very different person now from what he had been when first they met; but a glance showed that he was nearly at the end of his strength. At the back of Frank's mind was a dread that Mansfield's arm might go septic if he did not get rest and proper treatment, yet conditions made the one difficult and the other unobtainable. However, the first might be managed if they could find a village.

He threw a question to Mawanza.

"Yes, master, there is one not far from here where there are people of my own tribe. I was about to speak of it—see we must turn a little." He pointed slightly to the left.

They changed direction and entered a patch of dense jungle, watchful for any game-traps that might have been set by the local people to discourage animals from raiding their springing crops. At length the tangle thinned somewhat, and between the tree-trunks ahead they caught sight of the pointed tops of thatched huts, and heard the chatter of women busy with their daily tasks.

Mawanza stopped with a jerk and pointed suddenly to his right. Frank turned his head sharply. Among the trees that fringed the village clearing he saw what looked like a tent. As he stepped aside to get a better view he saw the figures of a couple of white men beside it, and the gleam of brass buttons and badges on their thin khaki tunics immediately proclaimed them to be troopers of the Rhodesian police.

With an exclamation of thankfulness, Frank and Mansfield turned towards them, Mawanza bringing up the rear with a broad grin on his face. As they came nearer the whole camp was revealed, with its group of natives—carriers and a couple of constables in red fezzes and blue tunics—squatting round the cooking-fire.

"Hallo! Hallo! Where have you sprung from?" began the taller of the two, whom Frank now saw carried a corporal's stripes on his sleeve. "We didn't think there were any other white men inside fifty miles or more."

Frank smiled feebly, for now that the strain was over he was feeling desperately tired. He jerked his thumb over his shoulder. "From over there," he said, "and pretty glad we are to see you, I can tell you."

"You look just about done in," the corporal commented. "Here sit down, and our boy'll be along in a minute with a brew of good strong tea that'll pull you together better'n anything." He produced a couple of folding camp-stools, and shouted an order towards the group round the fire, amongst whom Mawanza had already taken his place.

"We're doing the annual boundary patrol, y'know," he went on, "and ought to have finished before the rains broke, but we got delayed. Thank goodness we've finished now and are on our way back; we'll neither of us be sorry to have a good roof over our heads again, I can tell you."

The trooper, who hitherto had not spoken, nodded towards Mansfield's bandaged arm. "Hurt yourself somehow?" he asked.

"Yes, had a bullet through it."

"Bullet, eh? Bad luck! Done much damage? An accident, I suppose."

"By no means—very much the reverse."

The trooper raised his eyebrows, and the corporal whistled.

"Deliberate? Somebody had a shot at you? That sounds like something in our line."

"I wish you'd have a look at his arm," Frank put in. "I bandaged it up for him as best I could, but I'd none of the proper things."

"Luckily I have," the corporal responded. "Never go on patrol without 'em. Half a mo." He vanished inside the tent and quickly reappeared. "It wouldn't be the first bullet wound I've tended by a long chalk," he added, and Frank noticed the weather-stained medal ribbons on the breast of his tunic.

The rough bandage on Mansfield's arm was gently removed.

"It seems all right; quite clean and should heal up without complications," was the verdict. "Now just hold tight a moment, this is going to sting like blazes… That's better. Sorry it hurt a bit, but you don't want trouble later. Now for the lint and oil-silk and a bandage."

Deftly the dressing of the arm was completed, and the whole finished off with a neat sling.

"And now," said the corporal presently, when the strong refreshing tea had passed along its appointed paths, "what have you two fellows been up to, eh? Don't put it down merely to vulgar curiosity; you see, when two ragged-looking chaps appear out of nowhere, both beat to the world and one with a bullet wound, in our job it's only natural that we should sit up and take notice."

"It's a long yarn," Frank began.

"We've the rest of the day before us," came the dry comment. "We're not moving out of here till to-morrow morning."

"Well, then." Frank gave the salient facts about their journey up to the point where Oglethorpe had been unmasked, and dealt at greater length with events that had occurred since then. Mansfield, now lying down on an unrolled valise that the trooper had fetched from the tent, put in a word or reminder occasionally.

"Hmmm," the corporal grunted when they had finished; "so you've been shovin' your heads into a lot of nasty situations and got no benefit out of it all. I guess that Scotch friend you tell me about hit the nail fairly plumb on the head; you'll have to produce the man himself or an independent witness to swear identity before those legal chaps at home will be satisfied in the matter of your claim over the will. But you'll get it in time. When we fetch up somewhere where there's a wire we'll pass on what you say about this fellow, and when headquarters passes it on to the Portuguese police I expect they'll be only too glad to pull him in. You see, they'll have a definite charge—that of stirring up trouble and supplying arms."

"But that may take ages," Mansfield complained from where he lay. "These things are always as slow as you make 'em. We know he was close on our heels up to last night, and probably he's picked up our spoor again this morning and may be only a few miles away at the present moment. From what he said and hinted about that affair in the past in London, you ought to want him as much as the Portuguese. What about all of us going back on our trail and seeing if we can rope him in?"

The corporal shook his head emphatically.

"Sorry, can't be done. Apart from anything else, we've the strictest orders not to cross one yard beyond the border and enter Portuguese territory under any circumstances."

"But if he came over this side—"

"He won't. From what you tell me, the fellow knows well enough where his bread's buttered. But if he did—well, that 'ud be a different matter, I reckon. But it won't happen. Now about yourselves—I guess you'd better hitch on with us. We'll be starting back to-morrow morning and taking the shortest way, and we've plenty of stores and all that, so you won't be running us short."

Frank and Mansfield accepted thankfully, and talk turned to other topics until it was interrupted in an unexpected manner.

Meanwhile, what of Oglethorpe?

As soon as it had grown light that morning he had moved onwards. After some cautious searching he found the place where Frank and his companions had spent the night, for the crushed grass told its tale, and once more took up the spoor of boots that marked the damp soil.

He found the job easier now, for he was getting used to spotting the marks quickly.

Progressing steadily, at length he too reached the boundary pillar, and this brought him to a halt. Should he cross? he ruminated. Why not? The country was equally wild on either side of the border, and there would be no risk whatever. Besides, those he followed would probably relax their precautions now, thinking he would turn back. He visualised a neat surprise and a satis-factory ending. Yes, it was well worth going on.

A few yards beyond the frontier line he noticed where Frank and Mansfield had changed direction, and his hopes rose. He caught the sound of the distant crow of a cock and the high-pitched call of a woman. A village? That might prove awkward, but at least he could investigate.

Oglethorpe approached with infinite caution. He could see the tops of the huts, and then he saw something else to his right that brought him to an instant halt. Through a narrow opening between a huge baobab and a thicket of foliage he made out, silhouetted dark under the shadow against the sunlight beyond, the head and shoulders of Frank's seated figure.

From where he stood he saw nothing else, for the huge bole of the baobab hid the tent from his sight, and the thicket did the same for the natives round the camp-fire and the two policemen to whom Frank was talking. Mansfield he could not see, for he was lying down, but Oglethorpe knew he would be close by. Frank would do for the first shot, and Mansfield could be bagged before he had recovered from the surprise. An easy target, and at that range he could not miss. He raised his rifle and took aim.

Frank always contended afterwards that it was some subtle sixth sense that made him turn his head sharply at that moment. He glanced up the narrow natural passage between the baobab and the thicket, and saw Oglethorpe's tense and triumphant face and the levelled weapon. Instantly he threw himself backwards; as he did so the bullet whipped past where he had been a split second before, and the report of the rifle shattered the noontide silence of the forest.

The next moment the place was a whirl of movement. The two policemen sprang up, the corporal plucking the revolver from the holster at his belt and the trooper snatching up his service rifle. The native constables also leaped to their feet and grabbed their weapons, and a concerted rush was made for the spot whence the shot had come.

Oglethorpe saw the figures bounding through the undergrowth towards him, the sunlight that filtered through the leaves flashing on the tell-tale brass buttons and badges. With a gasp he realised what he was up against, and turned in panic-stricken flight.

After him raced the two white policemen and the uniformed natives. Frank scrambled upright again, snatched the shotgun, and followed, with Mawanza waving his spear and uttering blood-curdling yells bringing up the rear. A moment later the camp was empty except for Mansfield, who was trying to get to his feet without hurting his wounded arm, and the startled native servants.

Both the corporal and his mate were fresh and good runners, and Oglethorpe found them gaining on him. Like a coursed hare he jinked sharply, diving down a narrow tunnel amid the foliage. The pursuers pulled up with slithering feet and doubled after him.

Oglethorpe dashed along the leafy passage, head down and arms close to his sides. A moment later those behind saw his head jerk backwards and his feet fly out in front of him. With a crash he came to the ground.

In his wild rush to get away he had not seen that carefully concealed game-trap, and as his shoulders had encountered the hidden noose it had jerked itself tight round his neck. The speed of his flight had done the rest, and when his panting pursuers reached him, Oglethorpe was lying in a huddled heap with his head twisted at a grotesque angle to his body.

The corporal turned him over. "Neck broken," was his terse comment.

Frank nodded. "It strikes me," he said at length, "that the native who set that game-trap has done the hangman out of a job."

CHAPTER TWENTY

Two months had passed.

Some five weeks earlier, as soon as they had reached civilisation once more, Frank had seen Mansfield off in the mail-plane bound for England, and since then he had heard nothing from him. Not knowing where he would be, Frank had not been able to give Mansfield any address; but it was arranged that he should communicate with Mr. Larkman, the solicitor in whose office they had first met, as soon as he had any news.

Frank was now walking down the pavements of Manica Road on his way to that office, for he had had a message from Mr. Larkman telling him to call.

"Any news of Mansfield?" Frank asked as he took the chair that the solicitor offered him.

"Yes, I have had an air-mail letter this morning, and there's one for you too. He has proved his case and will get his legacy."

"Splendid!" Frank replied. "What does he say?"

Mr. Larkman picked up the letter from among his papers. "It's quite a lengthy epistle, and I'd better give you the gist of it. You remember how, at the time when Oglethorpe met his death, you urged those members of the Police Force who were present to make a detailed examination of the body, and note down all the marks and characteristics before committing the corpse to the earth?"

Frank grinned. "Yes, and the corporal wasn't half

sticky about it at the time, and the trooper none too keen. Said it wasn't their job to strip dead bodies, and go over 'em with a microscope; but they gave way in the end."

"Exactly. As I think you know, I procured from both of them sworn statements in writing which I forwarded to England. There were two scars of old injuries, you remember, and a peculiarly shaped birth-mark on the thigh. The doctor who had often attended Oglethorpe in the past was called in, and he promptly recognised the marks described on the affidavits of these disinterested witnesses. That settled it. Oglethorpe having been alive when they saw and chased him, he was therefore alive at the time the uncle died, and probate was issued accordingly."

"I'm glad. Mansfield certainly worked for his share. What about Oglethorpe's whack, by the way? Now he's dead, who gets that?"

"He died intestate—without making a will, you know. However, in such cases the Crown tries to be generous, and as, apparently, Mansfield is now his nearest living relation, a proportion will come to him."

"He seems to have struck it lucky all round," Frank commented.

"Yes, but he doesn't intend to keep that extra money. He says you've got to have some of that, considering, to quote his exact words, you've 'perishin' well earned a rake-off out of the doings.' In his letter he seems slightly excited and incoherent."

"But I hardly like to—"

Mr. Larkman placed his elbows on the desk. "Don't be a fool, young man. With his legacy on the top of what he has already, Mansfield will be very well off, and can easily afford it. The amount's not a great deal, anyway, though it's enough to set you up in any occupation you happen to fancy. I agree with him you deserve something beyond your wage, for if it hadn't been for you he'd have got nothing."

"Oh, all right; I'll accept gratefully."

"That's better. He says also that he hopes you'll use a bit of it to take a trip home for a holiday, so that, as he expresses it, 'we can have a good old beano or two in town together.' But I expect he says all that in his letter to you." The solicitor sought it among his papers and handed it over. "There's one other thing."

"What's that?"

"You had a native named Mawanza with you? Quite so; gone back to his village somewhere in the wilds, eh? Well, Mansfield wants you to get in touch with him and give him—no, not money, which I understand would not be much use to him out there—but quite an imposing list of somewhat er—strange gifts. I see the list includes a blanket and a large-sized shirt, knives and an axe, and other—er-desirable items. Will you see to this?"

"Of course," Frank answered with a laugh. "Mawanza certainly deserves setting up for life too. I'll hire a couple of really reliable natives to carry the things to his village. Anything else?"

"No, that's all. Read your letter, and if I can give any advice about the money when it comes, you have only to tell me. Don't bother to thank me—it would be unprofessional not to charge," he added with a wry smile. "As regards the suggested holiday in England, that's for you to decide; but after your experiences—" He ended the sentence with a gesture.

"I'll think about it," Frank replied, rising to leave and holding out his hand.